What people are saying

"Overall, Sister Margaret is wonderful start to this new series by the Myers siblings with its intriguing characters, nice sense of urgency, and satisfying conclusion."
-Zoe Williams. 8/10 Stars whatsbetterthanbooks.com -Best Book Blog 2017

"Sister Margaret is a slam dunk police procedural, giving the most on-the-money insider view of an investigation" …"if you are on the lookout for a new series of gritty police procedurals then Travis Myers and Natasha Myers Marsiguerra are definitely names to watch."
-DeathBecomesHer. crimefictionlover.com

"This really is a well-written novel that was an enjoyable and highly entertaining read."
-Nursebookie. 5/5 Stars Goodreads

"I really enjoyed this book! With just under 200 pages, you have a fast-paced plot, fully developed characters, and a wild glimpse into the life of an NYPD detective…I would suggest grabbing a copy of this book!"
-Brianas_best_reads. 5/5 Stars Goodreads

"The first book of the Tommy Keane series did NOT disappoint…I would definitely recommend this to anyone who loves a good police procedural."
-Laura's Reviews. 5/5 stars Goodreads

"This little gem of a novel…feels as though it could have been ripped right out of the newspapers"
-Kelly_Kills_Books. 5/5 Stars Goodreads

What people are saying about Hayden Jon Marshall~

"Devious, intense and disturbing! Hayden Jon Marshal is a twisty, action-packed, satisfying addition to what is undoubtably turning out to be a dark, suspenseful, compelling series by the Myers siblings."
-Zoe Williams, whatsbetterthanbooks.com

"Authentic and engaging crime fiction."
-Sandra Mangan, crimefictionlover.com

"One of the most intriguing, intense and suspenseful novels I have read in a long time."
Alison Owen. 5/5 Stars Goodreads

"Suspenseful and action packed! The writing is tight and the characters ring true. Highly recommended!"
Giuliana D. 5/5 Stars Amazon

"Oh my goodness they've done it again! Book number two of the Tommy Keane series is ABSOLUTELY BRILLIANT!!!!
Oriana Blyth, 5/5 Stars Goodreads

"Very Authentic! What a great read. I was hooked from the start. Cannot wait for the next in the series!
Betty Book Page 5/5 Stars Barnes & Noble.

"Great Detective novel…This is a must read for fans of crime fiction"
Tina Jackson 5/5 Stars Books A Million

What people are saying about Jenny Black ~

"NYPD Detective Travis Myers spent years "on the job" in the Bronx. Now, Travis and his sister Natasha, bring to life the escapades of fictional detective Tommy Keane in their latest fast paced police procedural."

-Pebody Award-Winning Investigative Reporter, Host of the True Crime Reporter Podcast, Robert Riggs.

"An exciting and interesting read, loaded with plot twists, and delightfully studded with punk rock references. Consider me an official Tommy Keane fan!"

-Suzie Que, Punkoleum Magazine

"Another great instalment, I have absolutely fallen in love with these books."

Crimegal 77, 5/5 Stars Barnes and Noble

"I'm becoming a huge fan of this series, and I've never been a series guy, but this one keeps me coming back for more!"

Just Joe, 5/5 Stars Goodreads

"NETFLIX, Make this a series already!"

Didi Arpayo, 5/5 Stars Goodreads.

LI JUN

Also by Travis Myers
&
Natasha Myers Marsiguerra

Sister Margaret

Hayden Jon Marshall

Jenny Black

LI JUN

A Tommy Keane Novel

Travis Myers &
Natasha Myers Marsiguerra

Published in the United States by Bully Press Corp.

Bully Press Corp
P. O. Box 404
Wingdale, NY 12594 United States
www.bullypress.net

Cover design by: Phred Rawles

ISBN- 978-1-7343370-9-9

For the clean-up team:

Mary, Rosemarie, Henry, Kristina, and Maryrose.

Rest in peace Rosemarie, you will be missed.

***

Dedicated to every Cop and Detective, in every city, in every country on the planet. Thank you for standing on the side of right, and for fighting the good and never-ending fight against those who would destroy all we hold dear.

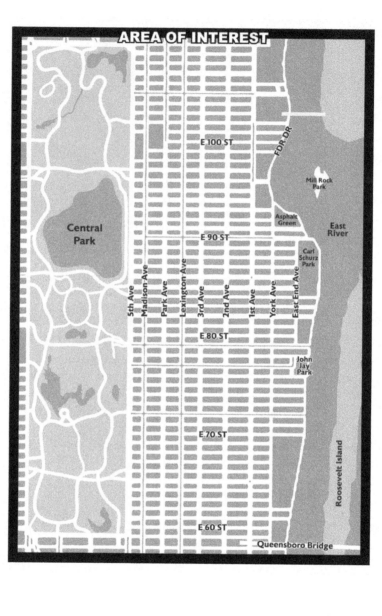

"When faced with what is right,

to leave it undone shows a lack of courage."."

~Confucius

Prologue

Growing up in Yorkville, Tommy was well acquainted with the Southerland sisters. Fiona, who was three years older than Tommy; Queenie, who was a few months older, and Amelia, who liked to be called Amy, was two years younger.

These three girls grew up in a small railroad apartment on East 87th Street between 1st and 2nd Avenue. Their father, Rodney, came to America from England as a roadie for the Rolling Stones. He loved New York so much that he decided not to return to London and went into self-exile as an illegal alien sometime around 1969. Rodney became an occasional cab driver, bartender, or mover; whatever he could do to earn a buck, keep a roof over his head, a scotch in his hand, and a joint between his lips.

In 1970 his girlfriend Millie, or Millicent, according to her birth certificate, joined him, and they were soon married at City Hall. Rodney and Millie were partiers; they loved and frequented all the bars on the East Side, drank heavily, and dabbled in drugs. Both made a living any way they could and their lifestyle, for the most part, was harmless to everyone but themselves.

Li Jun

New York City, by no means, was this couple's fall from grace, as they had enjoyed a hard drinking life in London as well, and personality wise, they were both suited for this life of theirs, as well as for one another.

Millie became pregnant and had their first daughter, Fiona. She was a lovely, healthy, bright child with blue eyes and flaxen hair, born just two days before Thanksgiving in 1972. The new parents attempted to raise her properly, but lack of money and poor lifestyle choices made both weak, and in general, neglectful parents.

Queenie, the Southerland's second daughter, was born in December of 1974. She shared her sister's blond hair, but had light brown eyes, rather than the sparkling blue eyes Fiona had. Her birth firmly drove a wedge between Rodney and Millie.

The added expense of a second child, the added responsibility that neither Rodney nor Millie could live up to, helped make for a very harsh, unhappy two years for all four of the Southerland's.

In early 1976, she became pregnant for the third time, and before the year was out, gave birth to the third Southerland girl, whom they named Amelia. Amelia was another beautiful, little, blonde baby, who shared the blue eye color of her eldest sister.

A month after Amelia's arrival, Rodney left. He took every cent the family had, which was barely anything, and caught a train to California. Never to be seen, or heard, from again, by any of the Southerland family.

Throughout the years, Millie continued to work, most often as a waitress, in a diner or a pub, and occasionally as a bartender. She desperately tried to raise her three girls on her own, while still attempting to also support her compulsive party life of drinking and drugging.

Her desperation for both cash and the nightlife, led to a revolving door of men in the Southerland's home. Some of Millie's male companions would last a few weeks, and others maybe a few months. Sadly, for Millie, and her daughters, she was never able to reconnect with anyone stable enough to be a good, healthy influence; nor anyone able to offer any sort of support, emotionally or financially, for her and her daughters.

Every man Millie had ever known was a taker, it was all she was all she was accustomed to, so it was all she ever expected. It was that simple.

The lack of a father figure, and the lack of any stability whatsoever in the home, led to a deficiency in education, and moral boundaries, for the Southerland sisters.

The eldest daughter, Fiona, grew to be the wildest of the three. She lost her virginity at age eleven, to the almost fifty-year-old Super of her building. Although this was a rape in the statutory sense, it was also the beginning of Fiona's life as a prostitute. She was not taken by force but rather was paid for the act, along with many, many, other sexual favors that would be sold to this man, and many more men, in the years to come.

Tommy, and his best friend Terry, acquainted themselves with Queenie Southerland in the seventh grade, their first year in Wagner Junior High School. The three of them shared their homeroom class, as well as several other classes throughout the week.

Queenie was, without question, the smartest girl in her family, and that included her mother, Millie. Even at an early age, she was always an intelligent and intuitive child. She was able to see things as they were and, as a matter of survival, by the age of nine became the most responsible person in the Southerland home.

The youngest, Amy, was a well behaved, but in contrast a rather dull child, who learned to follow Queenie as the leader of her household, simply because her sister was the strongest and brightest problem solver in the family.

Queenie would often steal from her mother in order to buy groceries for her sisters, she would also steal from Fiona, whenever she saw she had some cash. She knew that Fiona's money would be wasted on foolishness, rather than food or proper clothing. And of course, would pick the pockets of any, and all, of her mother's male visitors to the apartment – the never-ending revolving door of men who randomly appeared.

By the time she attended Wagner and met Tommy and Terry, Queenie was the acting head of the household; she did all the grocery shopping, the laundry, made sure the rent and bills were paid by her mother, which almost never happened on time, but managed to get done, somehow, month after month.

The three became fast friends while at Wagner, as they were attracted to one another due to their commonalities and street smarts.

Wagner was an odd school. It was situated on the Upper East Side at 220 East 76th Street and was made up of every different socio-economic class, race, religion, or status you could imagine. Extremely wealthy kids from Madison, Park, or 5th Avenues sat in class next to poor kids from any one of the housing projects nearby. Here is where these three, poor, working class, white kids from First Avenue bonded over similar likes and understandings.

Tommy and Terry grew close to Queenie, during the few years they spent together at Wagner, and slowly got to know her family and circumstances. As they did, they both realized the magnitude of how put-upon she was. Both Tommy and Terry were poor, of that there was no doubt, and both were raised by single mothers who had nothing but love to give their children. Seeing the way the Southerland sisters were raised was somewhat surprising, even to two rough and tumble street kids like Tommy and Terry.

The neglect of the Southerland girls left a mark on them both. They would often try to help Queenie and her sisters out with food, clothing, and cash whenever they could. Each would stick up for the three sisters anytime anyone on the street, or in school, would pick on or harass them.

Queenie left Wagner at fifteen, although she was one of the smartest girls in her class; she found work as a waitress at the Viand Coffee shop on 86th Street and worked there throughout what would have been her high school years.

Terry would end up in prison for the killing of a gang member in Julia Richmond High, at the age of seventeen.

Tommy would drop out soon after Terry was gone and join the Army. He became a paratrooper in the 82nd Airborne Division, also at the age of seventeen.

Tommy became estranged from the Southerland sisters, after he left for the Army, and only saw them around the neighborhood from time to time. Sometimes on the street or in the supermarket, and periodically he would run into Queenie, or her younger sister Amelia, in one of the several pubs he frequented during his twenties and beyond.

But it was a chance meeting with the eldest Southerland sister, Fiona, that would leave a scar on Tommy's soul.

It happened during a night of drinking with an Army buddy, Sergeant Mike Jarrel, who had come to see New York City for the first time, while they were still in the service. The two men left Fitzpatrick's pub located on 85th Street and Second Avenue. They stood on the corner, waiting for the light to change, so they could continue to their next intended stop, Ryan's Daughter, a pub located a block away.

Abruptly, they were approached by one of the prostitutes who worked 85th Street, between Second and Third Avenues, near the post office. She asked the two handsome paratroopers if they were looking for a date. The young men, who stood in uniform, at first ignored her. She became somewhat more aggressive …

"Come on, soldier boys … I'll suck both your cocks, just ten bucks each! … Come on, no one will ever suck you off the way I will … Just ten bucks each, come on."

Mike shyly laughed. He was a pleasant man who grew up in a small town in North Carolina and was surprised as well as a little embarrassed by this woman's advances. He asked Tommy if this was normal and happened all the time. Tommy also laughed. As he began to explain that there were prostitutes who worked this block, he stopped mid-sentence. His heart sunk and he lost his speech as he stared into the empty eyes of Fiona Southerland.

The nice buzz he had going, from the night of partying with his friend, had utterly been shattered. Yes, he knew Fiona was a wild girl. She had always run around with different men and had been drinking and drugging since she was twelve years old. He saw firsthand what a lousy life she, Queenie, and Amelia endured. But seeing Fiona like this, seeing her as a street walker, being approached and solicited by her, absolutely broke Tommy's heart.

He looked deep into her eyes, and she stared back, not knowing who he was. She was a mess, and although she was made up, she looked like something out of a horror movie. She was no more than twenty-three years old, but she looked like she could have been fifty. Her body was rail thin, her eye's had lost all sparkle, and were sunken into her head. Her teeth were no longer white, but a discolored mix of yellow and brown, and her hair was greasy and dull.

Tommy continued to stare at her unable to tear his eyes away. It was apparent that she was high. She stared back for a moment, and then finally spoke again.

"What the fuck, soldier boy? You want your cock sucked, or no?"

Tommy reached into his pocket and separated a twenty-dollar bill from the money he had and handed it to Fiona. Mike stood and watched the interaction unfold, and realized there was something to it, and remained a silent observer.

"Here... Please get yourself something to eat, and don't spend this on crack, okay?" Tommy asked, putting the bill into Fiona's hand, while holding onto it with both of his for a brief moment.

"What? What?" Fiona raised her voice with indignation. "What, you think you know me, motherfucker? You think you're better than me because you're in that uniform? Fuck you, cocksucker! Fuck you! You don't know me!" She continued to yell as Tommy and Mike crossed Second Avenue. She stuffed the twenty-dollar bill into her bra and continued railing more of the same foul language as the two paratroopers walked away down 85th Street, leaving Fiona on the corner.

***

Years later, while working as a patrol officer at the 5-3 Precinct in the Bronx, Tommy made it a point to know and befriend all the street walkers he encountered. His partner, Henry Sanchez, followed suit. Henry, never knowing exactly why Tommy had a soft spot for prostitutes, soon picked up on the fact that prostitutes, most all of whom were also junkies, had the saddest existence of just about any person on the planet.

Mostly, it was abuse that led them to prostitution and drugs. It was drugs and abuse that chained them to a life of prostitution. These women, and men, were truly the lost souls of society; abused, mistreated, scorned, and hated, even by the case workers of outreach programs who were supposed to be on their side and working for them.

For the most part these individuals were left completely alone in the world, with nothing left but to sell the one thing they owned... their bodies, in order to survive.

***

As is usually the case, positivity begets positivity. Simply by being kind and understanding to many of the street walkers in the 5-3 precinct, Tommy and Henry soon were on a first name basis. They built a professional relationship with many of the women who worked the neighborhood, especially where prostitution was most heavy and common, under the El Train on Jerome Avenue near St. James Park.

Tommy and Henry would regularly chat with these women, warn them to always be safe, and even give them a heads up if they knew Vice was planning a sweep on any given day.

In return, a few of these women would at random give information to the two officers that would lead to arrests. Getting some very dangerous individuals off the streets, people with guns who sold drugs and committed robberies.

Once, a pedophile was subsequently arrested by Tommy and Henry, because of their kindness to the most reviled people in society… the lowly crack-whore.

These destitute women were still human to Tommy, though forgotten and left to rot by society. Tommy knew they were the saddest victims of all.

Li Jun

Chapter One

Tommy's eyes opened to the early morning light dappling in through the lace curtains of Molly's bedroom. This was the fifth time they had gotten together in the last month.

Tommy would come into Bailey's Corner Pub for a drink and to read the paper while Molly bartended, then once her shift ended, they would grab a bite in a local restaurant, or perhaps head to another local gin mill for a few more drinks, before heading back to Molly's place for a night cap, some laughs, and of course some sex.

Tommy really liked Molly, but he knew there was no way this relationship would blossom into a real love connection for the two of them.

Molly was twenty-one years younger than Tommy, and if she had not almost forced herself on him four weeks prior, he would have never thought of approaching her for anything sexual. Sure, she was beautiful, young, funny, and intelligent, but their age difference and their lifestyles would never be compatible.

Tommy knew it and he knew Molly knew it. While he lay in bed thinking of all this, he looked at her naked body. He studied the muscles in her back which lay uncovered as she slept, her perfect white skin and her soft reddish blonde hair, and he began to feel lonely.

The emotion surprised him. It came on quick and forceful. She was everything most men, especially men Tommy's age, would want. For some reason, rather than feeling thrilled, this made Tommy feel even more alone. It wasn't just Molly making him feel this way, this revelation was a combination of everything happening, or not happening, in his life over the last few years.

By nature, he was a bit of a loner; not because he was antisocial, but those he regarded to be true friends were few and far between.

His oldest and dearest friend, Terry Callahan, who he loved and regarded as brother, had been estranged from him for decades. In part because of Tommy's job with the police department and his longtime desire to separate himself from the underbelly of his neighborhood, and in part because Terry's rise to become one of the neighborhoods most notorious archcriminals, made it impossible for them to remain real friends.

His longtime partner and confidant Henry Sanchez, who he loved every bit as much as Terry Callahan, suffered so bad from the injury that cost him an eye during a buy and bust operation while they were in Narcotics.

He rarely, if ever, left his home, and was now practically an invalid. Yes, they were still dear friends, and Tommy loved him, and his family with all his heart, but Henry's condition and inability to lead a normal and full life had removed Henry from Tommy's life to a large extent.

His divorce from Cookie, who he still considered to be his one true love, had left an irreparable hole in his heart. With the divorce came the limited time he was able to spend with his one and only child, his daughter Caitlin, who he absolutely adored.

Yes, his relationships with Cookie and Caitlin were excellent and full of love and respect, but he barely saw either of them. The fact that it was now an effort to do so for everyone involved made it so much sadder for Tommy.

He was happy to be spending more time at his mother's on 88th Street now, after his transfer from the 5-3 in the Bronx almost four months before. But, as much as he did love his mother, their relationship was not the kind to ebb the loneliness building in him.

This feeling, this odd feeling, that he was alone in the world and just a side note in everyone else's world had been building for some time.

It was on this particular morning, however, for no apparent reason, it decided to manifest itself. On a morning when he lay in bed with a young woman who was beautiful in every possible way.

***

Today was the first day back to work for the week. It was a little after seven in the morning, and he would be working the night shift, but he felt it was time to get up and start his day.

He quietly got out of bed and began to dress himself, as he did, Molly rolled over and opened her pretty green eyes and asked,

"You're leaving me sexy man? Where are you going so early?" in a soft sleepy voice.

"Yes, my sweet Molly, I have a few things I have to do today before I head into work later, I'm sorry to say."

"Noooo, don't go yet, come back to bed for a bit, and we'll grab breakfast later."

"I'm sorry honey, I got stuff I gotta do. Believe me, I'd rather spend the rest of today right here with you, but I can't."

"Okay, well you don't know what you're missing, I'm feeling in a particularly giving mood this morning." Molly grinned.

"No, no don't tell me that now, I don't want to be thinking about what I'm missing all day." He laughed.

"Yeah, well that's exactly what I want… I want you thinking of me all day and all night, and every day and every night, until you're back in this bed, I want you needing me… that's what I want, the lustful return of the sexiest man I know… so go ahead and leave me now but think of me…"

"You are so unfair miss Molly, and so fresh, but something tells me now that you've planted the seed that I *will* be thinking about you all day and all night." Tommy said as he pulled his sweatshirt over his head and reached for his jacket.

"Come here and kiss me before you go."

Tommy stepped over to Molly's side of the bed and leaned over to kiss her, as he did, she grabbed him by the lapels of his jacket and pulled him down on top of her.

As their lips met, she thrust her tongue into his mouth and held him there tightly for a few seconds. Molly got what she wanted because he would be thinking of her, and that kiss all day.

***

As it happened, Tommy had nothing to do for the day, but go to work in a few hours. But, for the few minutes he lay in bed with Molly, as she slept, that sense of loneliness had crept in and given him a sense of sadness and dread.

He recognized it wasn't fair be around her if he couldn't be there in the moment. Although her kiss did have him reconsider his decision to leave right then, he felt it was what he needed to do.

Tommy made the walk back to his mother's place on 88th Street and as he let himself in, he was greeted by little JoJo; the black and white Boston Terrier who had come into his mother's and his life, about nine weeks prior.

Little JoJo had grown considerably from the twelve pounds he weighed on the day he brought him to the ASPCA, after basically stealing him from a sign post he was tied to, on a freezing November night, to a solid very muscular twenty-three pounds.

"Hey, Ma, how you doing?" Tommy asked his mother, who sat in her recliner with the news on, smoked a cigarette and sipped a cup of black coffee.

"Okay, Tommy, and how are you, Tommy? You weren't here last night, Tommy, did you go home to White Plains last night, Tommy?"

"Yeah, Ma, I had some stuff to take care of yesterday, and it got late, so I just stayed up there. Sorry, I didn't want to call in case you had gone to bed." Tommy lied to his mother rather than tell her he was with Molly, because the conversation that was sure to follow, he would rather not have with her.

"That's okay, Tommy, I'm not keeping tabs on you. I was just curious, Tommy, that's all."

"Where's JoJo's leash, Ma? I'll take him out for a bit."

"I just had him out, Tommy, but I'm sure he would like a longer walk. I think the leash is on the counter, Tommy, check the counter."

"Yeah, I'll take him out and give him a nice long walk. Do you want anything while I'm out, Ma?"

"No, thank you, Tommy, I'm fine, Tommy."

"Okay, Ma, we'll be back in a bit, love you."

"Love you too, Tommy."

Tommy and JoJo stepped out onto the stoop. He scanned the block from left to right and headed out, while this odd loneliness clinged to him, as they walked slowly up the block towards 2nd Avenue.

He took in the doorways of each of the buildings he passed along the way, remembering the friends he had grown up with on this block as a child. Most all of whom were gone now.

He remembered all the elderly people who had passed over the years. People, who even if he didn't know them personally, he had seen hundreds of times, all of whom were gone now.

He remembered when Yorkville was still predominantly a working middle-class area, and when the streets were full of children as opposed to today when it seemed very few people in Manhattan stayed to raise their children.

Tommy stopped in front of the building Joey "JoJo no toes" Farrell had lived in and stood for a moment and had a few seconds of silence for Joey Farrell.

Joey died alone at the age of sixty-two, of a coronary right here on 88th Street in this same building in 2007. Although he was a beloved character in the neighborhood he was now lost to history and unknown to most of the people who now inhabited the block.

Tommy himself felt a bit like a dinosaur, a relic of the City's past, as he reminisced and recalled how Yorkville used to be. When everyone on the block knew everyone else, and people said hello; kids would help the elderly home with their groceries and would ask how you were and say strange things like; "Where you been? I haven't seen you for a while, how's your mother? How's your sister?"

Tommy understood things changed over time, he just didn't believe there was another time in history when things had changed as fast as they had in the last couple decades.

But then he also thought … maybe it was just him, maybe he had been so lost in his job for the last twenty years, the rest of the world had passed him by. Maybe he had been so wrapped up in needing to right the wrongs done by the most vicious of society, he lost his own path and forgotten to smell the proverbial roses along the way.

Was it possible he had fallen so deep into his own world of crime and criminals, and the subculture of the police department, that it was he who had left the real world behind, instead of the world leaving him?

As they walked around thoughts and memories swirled around his head. He had stories, so many stories, from his youth in this neighborhood, from his time in the army, from working in bars and clubs all around the city in his early twenties. All of them now just seemed like movies he once watched, all of them seemed so long ago.

He passed one of his old girlfriend's buildings on 90th Street. Rebecca Rivera, Tommy's first great love, they dated for about two years, until everything in their young lives changed dramatically.

After Terry Callahan was arrested for killing a boy in their high school's bathroom, Tommy dropped out of school and joined the army at the age of seventeen.

While in basic training, he received a letter from Rebecca telling him her mother had been diagnosed with cancer. Weeks later she had passed, and the next letter Tommy received from Rebecca was from her new home in Bayamon, Puerto Rico, where her father sent her and her younger sister to live with their aunt.

Tommy received a few more letters over the years, but never saw Rebecca again.

On this late morning walk he leaned against a parked car in front of her old building and thought of her. He remembered falling for her, thinking she was the most beautiful girl in Yorkville, how funny she was, how much she loved music, and how pleasant her family was.

He smiled at the memories of when they would sit on the stoop together, hanging out, and doing nothing. Terry would tell them stories about how they would rent an apartment together one day, be married, and have a son they would name Terry, because he was the best person in their lives. Tommy remembered how hard they would laugh at that, but also dreamt of it one day becoming a reality.

Now thirty years later he stood in front of Rebecca's old building and wondered what she did now, where she lived. She must have married. Was it only once? Did she have children? And how many? Tommy walked up the steps of the front stoop and into the vestibule and looked at the bell for apartment 2B. The name on the bell was now Heffernan, no longer Rivera, so no, her father, nor any other family member, was still living here.

'What the fuck, Tommy? What's the matter with you today? Feeling a little old? A little sorry for yourself?' He thought to himself. 'Well knock it off, life is good, and you have it way better than most. Quit your crying kid and get home and ready for work.'

He tried to reassure himself life was indeed good, and maybe he wasn't so lonely after all. Maybe it was just late-January post-holiday depression people were always talking about that had him off his game on this brisk January morning.

But whatever it was, he needed to shake it. Depression and self-pity weren't part of Tommy Keane's repertoire. He wasn't accustomed to it, and he didn't like it, so as suddenly as it had shown up this morning at Molly's place was how quickly he decided to cast it out.

Yes, the world had changed, and there was plenty he didn't like about its changing, but who was he to stop the world from spinning? There was nothing he could do about that but roll with the punches and continue on with his life. They headed home where they both took a short nap together before Tommy got himself up and ready for work.

Chapter Two

Tommy arrived at the 2-1 squad room about twenty minutes before his tour was to start, A-Squad was getting ready to leave now that it was end of tour for them, and Tommy said hello and chatted a bit with the detectives that were finishing up for the day.

He sat at Doreen Doyle's desk as he had for the last four months. There still wasn't an open desk available that he could claim as his own. Not that it really mattered. Sure, it was occasionally an inconvenience sharing a desk with Doreen, but the work always got done.

It also helped that Doreen, in Tommy's opinion, had turned out to be a total doll to work with and the arrangement they had was working as well as could be expected.

As the members of A-Squad began to file out, B-Squad began to file in. First to arrive, as usual, was Detective Mark Stein, then Lieutenant Kevin Bricks, Jimmy Colletti, Doreen Doyle, and Sergeant Brown all followed respectively.

The usual start of tour pleasantries were exchanged as Charice Tate, the squads PAA (Police Administrative Assistant), walked into the office with several case folders in her hands.

Li Jun

"Good afternoon, Detectives! Charice is happy to report that next to nothing happened in the ol' 2-1 today, nothing heavy anyway, just some small stuff that needs taking care of, a little cleaning up around the neighborhood that patrol never got to today." She stated as she dropped a new case folder on each of the detectives' desks.

Tommy opened his and read the 61 (Complaint report) for an aggravated harassment, in which a tenant complained that her super had called her three times during the night attempting to gain entry to her apartment to fix a leak in her bathroom that was raining down into her downstairs neighbor's place, and then returned that morning attempting to gain entry again and used foul language. 'My god... these fucking people,' he thought, 'Here is a guy trying to do his job and fix what sounds like a bad leak, and you're complaining about the inconvenience, and his language? This is not a police matter, and why the fuck didn't patrol squash this nonsense right then and there instead of wasting my time with this shit.' He shook his head and thought, 'I'll close this garbage with a simple phone call.'

"Anything pressing today, Tom?" Mark asked from behind his newspaper.

"No, Mark, I'm looking good this week, nothing big to contend with, you?"

"I'm in the same boat, have a couple open cases, but nothing serious. Doreen and Jimmy are headed downtown for a couple of subpoenas so it's me and you tonight, what say I'll take whatever   pops up first   and   you take whatever pops up second, if there is anything at all …"

"Sounds good to me. You want to grab something to eat right away, or give it a few hours?"

"No, I'm fine, let's give it a bit until we have a real appetite and then we'll decide what we want."

"Cool." Tommy said, as Sergeant Browne stuck his head out of his office.

"Who's up?" Browne asked.

"Tommy and I are, Boss, what do you have?"

"A call regarding a pretty bad assault just occurred over at the Carlow East Pub on Lex and 85th."

"Bad? How bad?"

"Not sure. I know they had to call a bus, looks like just one victim."

"Okay, Boss, we're on it and will let you know what's up."

"Very good, thank you."

"You want to drive, Tom?" Mark asked as he pulled his coat on.

"Sure, I'm liking this new Chevy Impala we just got, that old Crown Vic was on its last legs."

"Yeah, it was quite banged up, but we can travel in style my friend, so enjoy it while you can, this thing will be just as thrashed as the Vic before you know it."

Li Jun

***

6:08 PM
Carlow East Pub 1254 Lexington Avenue.

As Tommy and Mark pulled up to the Carlow East, flashing lights lit up the buildings and store fronts from the two patrol cars that sat parked in front. Tommy drove past and around them and then double parked just in front of where they sat.

As they climbed out of their car and approached the entrance to the bar, Sergeant Diaz stepped out of the door, buttoning up his jacket against the chill.

"Hi, Sarge, how you doing?" Tommy asked, extending his hand, "What you got for us?" He continued as the two firmly shook one another's hands.

"Hey, Keane, Stein, how you guys makin' out tonight? – We got a badly beaten Joey Macca. I know you got to be familiar with him, Stein, but if neither of you are, he's a well-known miscreant... petty thief, second story man (burglar) always into some kind of small-time shit."

"Yeah, I know him, I've collared him a couple times myself." Stein replied.

"Well, he's taken a serious beating here, bus just took him away a couple of minutes ago. He was unconscious when we showed up, and he looked bad."

"Is he likely?" Stein asked.

"No idea, the EMT's seemed concerned though... my man was in bad shape."

"What do we have for witnesses?"

"Two bartenders and four customers, everyone is inside waiting for you. Seems a big black guy came in, walked straight up to Macca, they had a few words and then the perp just beat him senseless, whole thing lasted just a few minutes."

"Any cameras?"

"Bartender says none that are working, they've been out of order for about eight weeks."

"Well, that sucks. Alright let's see what these wit's have to say."

***

Tommy listened intently, but remained silent, throughout the conversation Stein and Diaz shared. He knew Joey Macca personally.

He had known him for at least forty years, and Joey was exactly what Sergeant Diaz had described. He was a low-level criminal, and in general, a failure at anything and everything he ever attempted to do in his life. He was also a drunk and a pill-popping coke head. In his entire forty-seven years on earth, he had never held a meaningful job and was looked down upon by the entire neighborhood. He was thought of as a loser extraordinaire, even among the underbelly criminal class he associated himself with.

Li Jun

Tommy stepped into the bar and looked around. He was impressed. He had been to the Carlow East, many times, but not in many years, and it was obvious that the pub had gotten a full, proper, renovation since the last time he drank in the place.

Sergeant Diaz led them to the back of the pub where two pool tables were located. The two bartenders stood almost at attention behind the bar on their left. The four customers sat on stools against the wall, directly opposite the bar. Watching both the witnesses, and bartenders, were three uniformed officers.

On the floor, between the two pool tables, was a large amount of blood, most of which had oozed its way under one of the tables. The puddle was for the most part undisturbed but for where it was obvious that Joey Macca's head had been moved, most likely during the assault he underwent, as well as by his removal by the EMT's.

Both detectives examined everything in the room closely. They stared at the puddle of blood, looked around and under the tables for anything that may be a clue, or out of the ordinary. Each walked around the back area examining everything but saw nothing that grabbed their interest. Stein then motioned to the larger of the two barmen to come over to where they stood.

"Hey, how are you? I'm Detective Stein, 2-1 precinct. What's your name and what can you tell me?" he asked, staring over the top of his glasses at the fat, red-faced man. The man looked to be in his forties and was dressed in a simple, white button-down shirt, with a black tie, and black slacks.

"Hello, Detective, I'm Tony, Tony Makavic. I can't tell you much really… we had a decent crowd in, I heard some shouting, and by the time I got to the back, here by the pool tables, a big black fella was already darting out the door and the little white fella was bleeding all over the floor."

"And was he unconscious when you got back here?"

"Yes sir, out like a light."

"What happened between them?"

"No idea."

"You saw nothing?"

"No, sorry, nothing. Didn't even see the black guy's face, it all happened so fast, didn't notice the guy walk in, just saw him run out."

"Do you know the victim?"

"No, don't know him either. Sold him a Heineken, that's all I know about him."

"Okay, Tony, thanks. Go ahead back behind the bar and send your partner over here, please."

Stein asked the same questions of the taller, thinner, twenty something bartender who was dressed the same as Tony.

"Yes, ah yes, my name is Brian Smith, and no, no, I just saw a big black guy running out the door, didn't notice anything else… and no, no, I didn't know the little guy, just served him a couple, maybe three Heinekens tonight… I can tell you he was a cheap prick, and he didn't tip for shit, but other than that I know nothing about the guy."

The four onlookers basically all told the same story. Each of the patrons were older white men, aged between sixty and seventy and all claimed they didn't know the victim, or the perpetrator, but all agreed it was a large black man who ran out the door.

Once they made it through their initial interviews, Stein stepped away from the others to call the hospital, hoping to find out the condition of Joey Macca.

"He's in ICU and in a coma." He said to Tommy, ending the call and dialing the Crime Scene unit.

"You sure? No way, huh? Okay, well give me a name please... Hodges. Yeah, thanks." He replied into the phone.

"Crime scene is unavailable." he stated, as he lowered his phone and stuffed it back into his coat pocket.

"Ahh, well you know they would have had to have had nothing going on to show up to this one, no dead body, equals no Crime Scene."

"Yeah, it would have been nice though, now if this Macca kicks all I'll have are a few photos on my phone as evidence... Okay, we have everyone's info and statements, let's do one more look around, see if we spot anything unusual. Then we can head over to Lenox Hill and see what's up with Mr. Macca."

They looked all around again but found nothing of interest. They both took a few more pictures, thanked the bartenders and the customers, then departed the establishment.

Sergeant Diaz, and his driver, stood on the sidewalk near their car and called out a goodnight. As Tommy and Mark made their way back to their car a young, skinny, blonde woman of about twenty-five approached them.

"Excuse me? Excuse me? You are detectives, right?"

"Yes, Miss, we are." Mark answered.

"I... I saw that fight in there, I saw those men attack that man." She pushed her hair behind her ears and nervously looked around.

"You did?" Mark asked.

"Yeah, there were a bunch of people in there but after the fight happened the big bartender asked us all to leave, said he wanted everybody out of the place."

"Really? ... Interesting. Please dear, do you mind sitting in our car and telling us what you saw? Let's get out of the cold for a minute." Stein motioned to the Impala.

"Sure, absolutely."

Tommy unlocked the car and Stein opened the back door for the young woman.

"I'm gonna pull up the block so we're not in the middle of the street anymore." Tommy said and drove to the next block and pulled over in front of a fire hydrant. Mark shifted slightly in his seat so he could see in the back and began his interview.

"I'm Detective Stein, from the 21st Precinct, and what's your name?"

"I'm Kate Daniels, and I... I was having a drink with a friend from work, I'm sorry ... do you want me to tell you what I saw? Are you ready?"

"Yes, go ahead."

"Okay, so yes, I was having a drink with my friend Jenna, and these two men walked in. They came in kind of quick and aggressive to where that guy, the one who got hit was playing pool with some young Latino men, and they just started yelling at him, and then beat the shit out of him right there in front of us."

"*Guys*? So, there were two men involved?"

"Yes, two men, well really one did all the beating up... the other guy, the kind of scarier man just eyed all of us and made sure no one tried to stop what was happening."

"Can you describe these two men?"

"Yes, absolutely, the scarier looking man was maybe five-foot-nine, and looked about fifty, he had a grey jacket, with a black collar, the kind a construction worker would wear, but it wasn't dirty or worn like a construction man's jacket would be. He, he had salt-and-pepper hair, cut short, like a crew cut, or a flat top... He had navy pants and black shoes on, he was a tough looking man, with a scary scowl on his face, and the other guy, was also about five-nine, five-ten, younger looking but I would say at least forty, maybe forty-five, he had a black leather jacket on, like, just like the one you are wearing," she said looking at Tommy, "And he was the one who did all the talking and did all the punching, he had blue jeans I think, and white sneakers, he was also a very frightening man."

"And Miss Daniels, what... what color were these two men you just described."

"Oh. They were white, both white guys."

"Really... huh, could you make out what they were saying to him?"

"Oh yeah! They were yelling and cursing at him, do you mind if I curse?"

"No, no of course not."

"Okay, well, I can't stand by this exactly, but it was something like... and this was from the younger, thinner guy, the guy hitting the other guy... '*You motherfucker! You used my name? You cocksucker! Who do you think you are dropping my name?*' Mostly that. The guy who got attacked cried and pleaded but the other two weren't having it, and just punched that guy a bunch of times until he was out, you know, unconscious."

"Alright, thank you very much for coming to us. We must go to the hospital right now, but you so far have been the best and most interesting witness we have had today. Can I ask you to come down to the precinct to look at some photos later to see if you can identify the men who were involved?"

"Sure, I can do that, I will try anyway, it did happen really fast, but I can look at some pictures for you, sure."

"Okay great, Miss Daniels, please give me your contact information and I'll give you a call to set something up."

"Maybe tomorrow evening after work? I have plans already for later this evening."

"That sounds perfect, thank you. Where do you live, maybe we can we give you a lift home?"

"Really? Oh yes please, that would be great, 335 East 54th Street, if that's not too much trouble?"

"No, not at all, that's an easy trip for us… 335 East fifty-four, Jeeves." Mark said to Tommy in a sarcastic manner.

"Yes sir, Mr. Stein."

Tommy's answer was light-hearted, but he didn't like what they had just heard from this young woman.

The old men in the pub, with the old D&D (Deaf & Dumb) treatment, and the bartenders all agreeing it was some large faceless black man that came out of nowhere, then disappeared into the night, all while the surveillance cameras were fully out of order since Christmas, did seem a little convenient and a little too thin.

What really bothered Tommy, though, was the familiar sound of these two perpetrators that had just been described. Something rang a little too close to home with the young women's statement, and knowing Joey Macca, and the circles he ran in, left him a bit uneasy.

'Could it be? Would it be? … No.' Tommy pushed the thought out of his mind. He would let the case lead them to wherever it led, but he wasn't going to worry or stress over maybe's or might-be's. Besides, he thought Joey Macca would be able to tell them who beat him. Whether it was two white men or one black man, Joey Macca would, or should, know his attacker.

***

Travis Myers & Natasha Myers Marsiguerra

After dropping Kate Daniels off at her building, Tommy and Mark headed back up to Lenox Hill Hospital on East 77th Street, to check on the condition of their victim Joey Macca.

"So, we have six witnesses telling us one large, black, perp beat our Mr. Macca half to death… and one   small,   female witness telling us a completely different story of two very scary white   men   beating our Mr. Macca half to death… and with considerably more detailed information and descriptions… Me thinks there is a little something amiss here with these different stories there, Tom."

"Yeah well, I think we got an old school case of D&D in the Carlow East, and it's coming from both sides of the bar."

"Yeah, I think you're 100 percent on that, Both the staff and those old timers are Deaf and Dumb, and want to stay away from this one for some reason… all's I can guess is that our perp, or perps, doing the beating are probably known to some, if not all, of those people in there."

***

At Lenox Hill, they spent a few minutes trying to track down an available nurse at a station. Once they did, they were told that Joey Macca had been admitted and given a bed in the ICU and that Macca was indeed in a coma due to his injuries. The nurse stopped an older woman in a white coat, that was walking by, to tell her these detectives were asking about Macca.

Dr. Edith Lunfeld gave them a complete rundown of the injuries stating that Macca had severe swelling in his brain due to the trauma of the beating he had taken. That's what caused him to slip into a coma which she currently believed was not life threatening. She had no way of knowing for sure when Joey Macca would awaken but did think he had a good chance of recovery given the circumstances.

When Stein asked a second time, "He will live though, yes, Doctor?"

Dr. Lunfeld replied, "There is always a chance he may not ever recover, but I believe he will. Only time will tell, Detective, but I would imagine Mr. Macca will recuperate. He arrived here very quickly after his injuries. Had it been longer, he may not have fared so well, and if we had received him just a few minutes earlier you would most likely be speaking to him right now... all that said, we will have to wait and see, but I do believe with a little time, he will mend."

As Stein thanked Dr. Lunfeld a call came over the radio.

"2-1 squad, 2-1 squad patrol requests an 85 forthwith to 439 East 80th Street for a DOA, possible jumper."

Tommy answered, "10-4 central, 2-1 squad enroute to location."

"10-4 2-1 squad enroute."

"You got that, Mark, we got a possible jumper, DOA, over on 80th."

"Okay, let's go," Mark said, then looking back at Dr. Lunfeld, "Here is my card, Doctor. Please notify me of any progress Mr. Macca makes, and of course, if he takes a turn for the worse."

"Yes, Detective, I certainly will."

Chapter Three

9:22 PM 439 East 80th Street.

Tommy and Mark drove up 1st Avenue and found patrol to have run police tape across the street on 80th where they were going to turn. Officer Ortiz immediately recognized Tommy and Mark, as they attempted to make the turn, and lifted the tape as high as she could so that their car would fit under it, and they could continue down the block towards the flashing lights of the awaiting patrol cars.

Halfway down the block, Tommy pulled in front of the Caedmon School, the first Montessori school established in New York City. The school sat on the southside of the street, opposite, and a few buildings up, from 439. As they approached the flashing lights, they once again saw Sergeant Diaz, who from about fifteen yards away, motioned in the direction of 439 with his head. Tommy and Mark looked in that direction and viewed what appeared to be a sheet covering a body that was impaled on a wrought iron fence.

Once they stepped a few feet closer they realized that was indeed exactly what they were looking at.

Sergeant Diaz began, "Rios and McCartney were right there across the street," Pointing with his hand to the building the officers had come from. "They had a domestic call and just as they were leaving the building, this woman came down from above and landed on this fence… They said they heard her land and then looked over and saw what had happened. As they walked across the street towards the scene several people began to exit the building, they grabbed all but one who was already halfway down the block, they sat everyone down on the hallway floor until I arrived. We have eight people total, five Chinese, one man, and four women, and three Caucasians, one of which is Hasidic. It appears this is a Chinese massage parlor, more likely a brothel, and we have several staff and clients running out of the building just after this young woman," Diaz tilted his head toward the covered body, "Came out of the third story window landing on this black iron fence here."

Tommy stepped closer to the body. The sheet draped over her did little to hide the spikes of the wrought iron that had penetrated and protruded right through the young woman's body, which hung lifeless. Tommy glanced up at the building and estimated the window she fell from was some thirty plus feet above.

Tommy stood silent for a moment, then gently lifted the sheet, so he could examine the corpse that hung beneath it.

The young Asian woman could have been in her twenties or possibly still a teenager. She wore nothing but a thin see-through, pink lace teddy. Her jet-black hair was tied into two pigtails with matching pink elastic bands. She was exceedingly small, possibly weighing less than a hundred pounds.

Tommy leaned down to get a look at her face; she was pretty, her face fully made up and her eyes were open, staring back into Tommy's.

"Ahh, you poor dear thing." Tommy said softly to her.

As Mark and Sergeant Diaz watched Tommy examine the young woman's body, Sergeant Diaz informed Mark that he had already put in a call to the Medical Examiner's Office, and to the Crime Scene Unit, who said they would be delayed.

"Delayed?" Mark said flatly, "Well at least they're coming. We called them for that assault earlier at the Carlow, in case our victim kicked, and they said they couldn't make it at all."

"Hope you got a name from Crime Scene… and how's that Joey Macca doing? He gonna make it?" Diaz asked.

"Yeah, I got a name. Looks like he will. He's in a coma, the doctor says he should survive, but unknown when, or even if, he'll awaken…"

Tommy stepped forward and interjected himself into the conversation.

"Okay, so looks like we have an Asian prostitute, who fell, jumped, or was thrown, out a third-floor window to her death. Eight civilians and two members of the service to interview. Overheard you say you notified crime scene and the M.E. – Thanks for that, Sarge, we appreciate it." Tommy put his hands on his hips and blew out a breath. "Well, it looks like we got hours of work ahead of us, Mark, let's take a look at what's going on in this building. And I guess, fuck me… I guess we'll take all these people back to the station house and do our interviews there."

"Yeah, that's going to be our best bet. We'll have to separate all of these people also, especially all the Chinese, we don't want them putting stories together and agreeing to them before we have a chance to interview them individually… we're going to need some help from you, Diaz, do you think you can get us a couple cars, or a van, and some people to transport and babysit, until we can get with each of them? We'll, of course, have the rest of our team over here but there are a lot of folks to transport here." Mark asked.

"Absolutely, not a problem, Detective, even if it takes us a couple of trips."

"Thanks, Sarge, that's a great help," Tommy replied, "In the meantime what say we separate these people here in the hallway, as best we can. Then, you and I, Mark, will go do a walk through the apartment this young woman came from. If you would, Sarge, have either Rios or McCartney keep an eye on our victim here, and the others keep the crowd in the hallway quiet. Keep them seated on the floor, a few feet away from one another, so like Mark here said they don't cook up some stories."

"Got it, we'll do what we can to help." Sergeant Diaz replied, then turned and barked at Officer Rios, who was on the stoop. "You got that Rios? You keep an eye on this victim here." He stepped up the steps of the stoop and then barked at McCartney, "McCartney – move all these people, so they are about five or six feet apart, and no talking! You hear me people? All of you, please, shift yourselves over, I don't want anyone to close to anybody else, and no talking… is that understood? No talking to one another! In a few minutes we will begin taking you, a few at a time, over to the 21st Precinct to be interviewed by detectives. We don't want you talking to one another until you are interviewed, am I clear? Does everyone understand that?"

"Excuse me, Sergeant, isn't that some sort of violation of our rights?" The Hasidic man spoke up.

"No, it's not! You're being held pending an investigation - And you should have thought about being inconvenienced by the police before you came here to get your dick sucked!" Officer McCartney snapped back.

"What kind of a way is that for an officer to talk to a tax paying citizen?" The Hasidic man asked.

"Shut up, he's right!" Sergeant Diaz replied, "Now all of you, no more talking until a detective is asking you questions... that's it, no more!"

Tommy and Mark slowly walked past the eight people lined up in the first-floor hallway of the building. As each got their first glimpse of these people they took in as much detail as they could.

All five of the Chinese sat silently, with their heads hung low, starring into their laps. There were three young women, who all appeared to be in their early twenties. The girls all had coats on, but their legs were bare, and all three wore high heeled shoes. The fourth woman was an older Chinese woman. She was heavy set, and appeared to be short, very overweight, and possibly forty or more years of age. She was well dressed, nicer than any of the others, and her clothing appeared to be high quality. She wore large gold earrings, a gold chain around her neck, and gold rings on each of her fingers.

Next to her sat an older Chinese man with a receding hairline and black framed glasses. He wore simple black slacks and a white button-down shirt. The Hasidic man, who sat next to him, was about forty years old. His glasses had thick, black frames and he was dressed in traditional Hasidic garb. He looked up at the detectives as they passed, and just as he spouted off to

Sergeant Diaz and Officer McCartney, about his rights, he continued his rant towards them.

The other two Caucasian men sat quietly. One, who also appeared to be about forty, was dressed casually in jeans and a black and red flannel shirt. He kept his eyes shut and his head leaned back against the wall. The other man, who appeared to be about fifty, was dressed in a grey suit and tie, and wore an expensive looking black wool coat. He stared straight ahead, through his wire framed glasses, at the wall ahead of him, not making eye contact or speaking to anyone.

The two detectives reached the third floor. There were four doors to choose from, but they were pretty-sure the one they wanted would be the one towards the front and on the left side of the hallway, because of the positioning of the window the victim came from, it simply made sense. With a turn of the knob all doubts were lifted, as the door was unlocked. Once open, the set up was obvious to both Keane and Stein, that the apartment was being used as a brothel.

The door opened into a room, that would normally be used as a living room and kitchen combo, but in the kitchen area, sat a desk and a chair. Opposite the desk, eight simple black metal folding chairs, lined up against the wall. To the right of this room there was a door left wide open. It led into what was once a small bedroom with two windows, which was now divided down the middle by sheetrock, making two very small spaces. Each niche was only about six feet wide, by eleven feet long. At the end of each was a window. The window in the room to the right was closed, and the shade was drawn, and led to the fire escape. The window in the room on the left was wide open, the shade was up, and it was obvious that this was the room where the young woman's body, still hanging on the fence below, had come from.

Both rooms were sparsely furnished. A twin bed, with a simple white fitted sheet, and no blankets, against one wall and a small dresser and chair against the other. The two dressers had a bowl full of condoms and a plastic bottle of K-Y Jelly on the surface. The walls were bare white, without any art or decoration, adorning them. The entire place held a sickening sweet odor of perfume and sweat.

The detectives slowly walked through and examined each room silently, without touching anything, then made their way back into the front room with the desk and chairs and did the same. Past the front room was a small bathroom, which they each entered and examined separately because it was simply too small to be in together. Then they opened the last remaining door in the apartment. This led to another room, that again had been divided into two, very small, six by ten-foot rooms, and were appointed exactly the same as the rooms in the front with a twin bed, a small dresser, and a chair.

"Alright, nothing to do here now until Crime Scene comes and does their thing... and it looks like that may be awhile. So, what do you think? You want to get all these people over to the precinct and have Doreen and Jimmy start questioning them?" Mark asked.

"Yeah, we're gonna have to, this is going to be a cluster fuck of an investigation, I can see that already." Tommy replied as he pulled out his cell phone and made a call to Lieutenant Bricks.

"Hey, Lu, how you doing? Listen, we have quite a mess over here on 80th Street, no idea if this is a suicide or a homicide, it could easily be either, and I have eight possible witnesses and/or perps… what's that? Yeah, it appears to be an Asian brothel on the third floor of a walk up… it's at 438, no sorry, 439 80th… You think you can grab Doreen and Jimmy and come give us a hand? … Great, thanks, yeah see you in a bit… also Lu? Could you do me a favor and put a call into the Asian Gang Unit for me? I don't have their number and I'm sure they'll probably want to do some interviews once we're done… Yes sir, yeah Lu, thanks."

"Alright, looks like we have some work ahead of us there, Detective." Mark said as soon as he heard Tommy finish his conversation.

"You got that right, let's head downstairs and wait for the others." Tommy said, just before walking back over to the open window, where they believed their victim came from. Cautious not to touch anything, he placed his hands in his pockets. He looked all around the window trim, sill, and floor, for any kind of clue, then stuck his head out the open window into the cold. He stared down for a moment at the woman impaled on the fence below. Tommy took a deep breath of the cold crisp air and said softly to her, "We'll figure this out, young lady, and if there is a debt to be paid, I'll do my best to collect it for you."

He quietly left the room and he and Mark made their way out of the apartment and down the stairs to the front of the building.

On the last flight of stairs, Tommy slowed his pace slightly, and eyed each of the individuals who still sat on the floor. All the Asians still had their heads down, staring at their laps. Two of the Caucasian men had their heads leaning back against the wall, with their eyes closed, as did the Hasidic man, until he heard Tommy and Mark make their way down the stairs and then he began to speak.

"How much longer will you be holding us here, Detectives?... Detectives? How much longer? This cannot be right, Detectives, holding us here against our will... this is an outrage, do you hear me?"

Tommy and Mark remained silent as they walked towards the door of the building, slowly perusing the eight people they had in custody, as they passed them by. Once out the vestibule door and on the stoop, McCartney could be heard, "Alright! That's enough out of you, no more noise until a Detective is asking you questions, you got that!" he barked bitterly.

It wasn't even another three to four minutes until Lieutenant Bricks, Detective Doreen Doyle, and Detective Jimmy Colletti, arrived on scene. The three of them chatted with Tommy and Mark and it was decided that Doyle and Colletti, along with Lieutenant Bricks and some officers from patrol, would remove the eight individuals they had in custody to the 2-1 Precinct. They would begin preliminary interviews of each of them and hold all eight at the station house, until Tommy and Mark were able to return and re-interview everyone involved.

Once the eight were off to the station house, Tommy and Mark began a door-to-door canvas of the building, in search of any other witnesses. Then they would canvas the three buildings across the street, in the event there could be someone who may have seen something, from their window.

As Tommy said earlier, they had hours of work ahead of them. They began with the first floor and made their way up to the top. There were two apartments per floor, and five floors, leaving them nine apartment doors to knock on, of which four there was no answer.

Of the remaining five apartments three heard, saw, or knew nothing. Mr. and Mrs. Polchinski had the most to say, they lived in apartment 2A, just below the massage parlor/brothel.

"Listen, we have complained about these people in the past, both to the building management and to you, you the police. We knew these people were up to no good, all day and late into the night, people coming and going from that apartment... It's illegal, even if it is just massages and acupuncture, it has to be illegal to operate a business this way out of an apartment like that... it has to be! Tell me I'm wrong!" Mr. Polchinski declared. He was a small, older man in his seventies, bald, and dressed casually in blue pants, held up by blue suspenders, over a simple white t-shirt.

His wife was equally annoyed, "Really, Detectives, we honestly have complained about this before, and now look, just look what has happened! A girl is dead, I mean my god, a young girl is dead, because of some illicit happy ending massage business here in a residential building... I mean really, Detectives, this used to be such a nice building and now we have what? What I ask you? Criminals, that's what! Criminals right over our heads... disgraceful... it's absolutely disgraceful."

Tommy listened intently, apologized profusely for the lack of police attention, and promised he would be speaking to the landlord about this. But sadly, other than the complaints the Polchinski's had, there was nothing of value to add to the investigation, so he moved on.

Another elderly man, Mr. Bundy, who lived in apartment 3B, right across the hall from the apartment in question, also had plenty to say, and this time it was a bit more valuable.

"Yes, yes, yes, Detectives, these people have been renting here for just about six months, but no one lives in that apartment. They just do business out of it. Every morning at about 9-9:30, a white van shows up with the same man... older fella, seems to be about fifty-five, maybe sixty, and three to six women... they're all Chinese, he is... well, he's the boss but more like a manager I think, and the women, hell -- women, some of them are just kids, just teenagers, well they're all pro's, you know... Prostitutes. People think it's a massage parlor, but it's not, they're running a whorehouse next door, it's that plain and simple, see. They show up at 9-9:30 then all day men are in and out of there until about 10:30-11 at night, then the white van comes by and picks them all up." Mr. Bundy explained.

"This is some great information Mr. Bundy, now tell me sir, what makes you think this older gentleman is the manager?" Tommy asked.

"Well, Detective, mostly I just feel it, but you see I'm here all day, every day, I see them come in the morning and go in the evening, and he is always dropped off with them... The women that is, they all come upstairs here, and the van doesn't leave until he gives them a high sign from the window... I guess to let the driver and his helper know it's okay... there are always two men in the van, you see, and they don't leave until they get the go ahead from the older fella... So yeah, he seems to be the boss. That is, until the fat woman, and or the stocky kind of well-built man show up, when they come it's either in a nice car or a cab, and both are definitely bosses of some kind. She shows up almost daily, sometimes twice a day, and I think... I don't know

now, I just think, she shows up to collect the money, and occasionally dole out some discipline."

"Discipline?" Tommy asked, "Please tell me more?"

"Well, I've heard her yell a few times, and even once saw her slap the older fella in the hallway here through the peep hole, and he didn't move a muscle, he just took it... So yeah, I think she is his boss... Also once, a few months ago I think, now again Detectives, I think... I don't know, but it sounded like she, or someone, was beating on one of the girls in there. It was all muffled through the walls, but that's what it sounded like to me. There was yelling in Chinese, and some banging around and screaming, only lasted a minute but it was noticeable."

"Have you heard that often?" Mark asked.

"No, no, overall, they are surprisingly quiet, especially with all the people who are in and out of there all day, but you can hear people doing it... You know... having sex, not constantly but daily, mostly it's from the men, you know the customers, the Johns, they make the sex noises... The women rarely make a sound... The most annoying thing is you can hear the buzzer from the intercom go off all day, and you know it's not that loud, and it's muffled, but it's all day, twelve, thirteen hours a day."

"What did you hear or see tonight, Mr. Bundy?" Tommy asked.

"Some yelling and screaming, it was a bit aggressive and unusual, so I got up from the TV and looked out the peep hole and saw everyone leaving in a rush."

"Everyone you say, can you describe them to me?"

"Oh, uh gee, let's see, first was a big guy in one of those navy pea coats, then the Chinese, one by one, and then three white men, one with glasses, and one was a Jewish fella."

"Thank you, and…" Tommy began but Mr. Bundy interrupted him.

"The first fella, the big one with the pea coat I recognize from the Liquor store on Second Avenue, he works there a few days a week."

"Really, now there's some information, do you know his name?"

"No, sorry Detective, that I don't know."

"Thank you so much for your time, sir, we appreciate it. Can I ask you, just one more thing, do you know any of the names of the Chinese? Can you help us out with that at all?" Tommy asked.

"No, sorry, I hear them all day, but it's all Chinese, I have no idea what they're saying, I'm sorry, Detective."

"No, no problem, thank you very much, Mr. Bundy, we appreciate it. You have my card, sir, if you think of anything else or learn anything else, please don't hesitate to give us a call."

"Yes, yes I will, Detective, and thank you."

***

Once the detectives were done with that building, they made their way across the street and rang some bells and knocked on some doors, but nothing of value was learned. The few people they were able to speak with saw and heard nothing until the police arrived with their flashing lights and had more questions for Tommy and Mark than answers.

They returned to 439 and waited another 30-40 minutes before the Medical Examiner arrived. Both Tommy and Mark recognized the woman walking toward them, ME Kristen Smyth, and both were happy to see her on the case. She was bright, usually full of energy, and always very thorough, informative, and willing to help.

"Hey, ME Smyth, how you doing?" Tommy asked.

"Very good, Detective Keane, Detective Stein, how are you gentlemen this evening? So sorry it took me so long to get here, the city is hopping tonight."

"Not a problem, we certainly understand. Unfortunately, Crime Scene has yet to arrive, it's obviously a busy night for them as well. We put a call into them a couple hours ago for another job and they couldn't make it." Said Mark

"Wow, well yeah, like I said it's a hot one tonight. I have to head up to Washington Heights, as soon as I'm done with you here, we have one dead and another likely waiting for me, luckily for you, you're on my way – Okay -- Wow, this looks awful, what happened? Was she a jumper?"

"We don't know, Ms. Smyth, we believe she was a prostitute, and she either jumped from that open window there on the third floor with the light on, or possibly was thrown out, but we have no way of knowing anything just yet."

"Okay, well she's certainly dead, let's remove this covering and have a look at her body, ooh, ouch! What an awful way to go, damn, this is bad."

Kristin Smyth continued to speak as she removed the victims cover and examined the body as it hung over the iron fencing.

"Okay, well she's still soft so it's obvious she hasn't been here very long."

'No, we know she died at approximately 21:10 hours. We actually had two uniforms across the street here when it happened." Tommy said.

"Really, what are the chances of that, so they actually saw her jump or fall?"

"No, they heard her land, then looked over and saw what had happened. Yeah, talk about luck, they were able to grab eight witnesses, possible perps, who were looking to leave the scene." Tommy answered.

"That is some luck for you guys, isn't it? I won't be able to touch much here until Crime Scene gets done doing their thing, but let's see what we can see before they arrive," as she began examining the victim. "Okay, looking at her nails, I can't immediately see any flesh under them, that doesn't mean I won't find any at the autopsy tomorrow, please make sure Crime Scene bags them for me."

"Of course." Tommy replied.

She continued to examine every bit of the young woman's body as it still hung on the fence, then made her way up a few steps of the stoop and climbed over the handrail in order to get to the other side of the tall wrought iron fence. She continued her examination of the lower half of their young victim's body.

"Okay, yes, she has certainly had sex recently, and I can be pretty sure she has had both vaginal and anal penetration sometime within the last few hours. No surprise there of course, we do believe she was a prostitute, correct?"

Neither Tommy nor Mark answered since it was a rhetorical question.

"Looking here, this young woman also has some tell-tale signs of abuse connected with her profession, you see she has scars from cigarette burns in between her toes, and there are also a few just below her hair line… See, you can see them there."

She said as she put her arm through the bars of the fence and pointed at the victim's hairline.

"She has been punished or tortured by her pimps/captors, who didn't want to scar or disfigure their beautiful property. That's why they burned her where no one could see… I know you guys are waiting for Crime Scene, so we can't do much more here right now. My initial examination here won't give us much more than I've already told you, so leave her where she is until Crime Scene shows and does their thing, then my guys will bag her and remove her to the morgue. I'm thinking I can have her autopsy done by tomorrow afternoon, whichever one of you is the investigating officer can come see me around two or three if that's cool, I should be close to done by then. Maybe give me a call first, but I think we should be good to go by that time."

"Very good, it will be me, and that time frame is perfect." Tommy replied.

"Alright, Detective Keane, I look forward to it." ME Kristen Smyth said, as she handed him her card and he handed one of his to her.

Shortly after ME Smyth left, Crime Scene rolled onto the block. Then spent about ninety minutes photographing and measuring and documenting everything there was to document about the scene, on the street level where the body hung.

Once they were finished, the techs from the ME's office took on the gruesome task of removing the body from where it hung on the fence, placed it into a black nylon body bag, and took it to the morgue.

Tommy and Mark then returned to the apartment where they slowly, and methodically, searched each room one by one. They recovered $6,280 in cash, two cell phones, a Samsung Galaxy tablet, a small plastic zip lock bag containing 102 white tablets, and a small black .9mm Taurus handgun. All of which they removed as evidence, after having Crime Scene photograph and document where everything was located in the apartment.

By the time they had finished and returned to the precinct it was 1:54 in the morning.

Li Jun

Chapter Four

Arriving at the precinct Tommy and Mark had a short sit down with Lieutenant Bricks, Detective Doyle, and Detective Colletti, to discuss what Doyle and Colletti had learned during their initial interviews of all the witnesses. And receive their DD-5's (Complaint follow up reports) to add to Tommy's quickly growing case folder.

As they sat in the squad room, Tommy began, "So what did we find out, do we have any idea what happened to this young girl?"

Lieutenant Bricks was first to speak up, "Well, it would appear all of our Johns were seated and awaiting their turns with the girl of their choice, please interrupt me if I misspeak here you two," He said, directing that last bit towards Doreen and Jimmy, who actually conducted the interviews, "They were more forth coming than any of the Asians, who have remained fairly closed mouth thus far... anyway, it seems a John that we don't have here, that left before we were called to the scene, had some complaints about the young woman who has now passed, and from what you'll read on these DD-5s here, at first the older, Asian man stepped into the room, her room? And yelled at her in Chinese... I think we agree, right? These are all Chinese people here, correct?

"Yes, Lu," Doreen answered.

"Right, and so after the older Asian man left the room, the larger older woman went in with the john who was complaining and confronted our victim, from what all three of our johns say, they heard her scream at the girl. Then heard what sounded like some slaps, some more screaming from both women, and then the John ran out of the room and out of the apartment, and the older woman ran out of the room, grabbed her coat and bag, while screaming in Chinese at the old guy and the other girls, they all took flight out the door and down the stairs, where everyone we have here were grabbed by Officers Rios and McCartney as they exited the building."

Lieutenant Bricks paused, and took a deep and tired sounding breath, then continued.

"All five of the Chinese have been less than helpful, they are all claiming no English, however all three of our Johns confirm, as far as they know, all of them do speak English, now as far as our johns go… We have promised them nothing, but told them if they cooperated, they most likely will be on their way home tonight, and we won't be putting anyone through the system or contacting any wives or families, again, as long as they cooperate… and to your satisfaction. From what I've been told, and read in these DD-5's, they do appear to be cooperative and are yours until you are done with them, Tom… How's that? Did I miss anything?" Lieutenant Bricks ended his summary again directing his attention to Doreen and Jimmy.

"No, that's about it, Lu, I will add that the guy in the flannel seems to be the easiest and most forthcoming, his name funny enough is John -- John Donner, and he's pretty easy. I also spoke with the guy in the suit and tie, Jacob Blake, he's a little more uptight, but certainly not difficult. He's fifty-three, and married, from East Patchogue Long Island. I think he's given us everything he can, really both I think have, but that will be for you to decide, and both were easy... I tried talking to each of the women separately, and so far, no luck with any of them. I did notice what appeared to be a scratch on the wrist of the older, heavy one, consistent with what I would guess is a fingernail."

"Good lookin out, thanks, Doreen."

Jimmy then added, "I had the Hasidic guy, he started out as a bit of a dick but has relaxed a bit. Once he realized this could be a murder investigation, he spilled everything he knew, and actually told me he has frequented this particular brothel exactly four other times, and his story matches exactly what Doreen's two interviews stated -- some yelling, screaming, slapping, and then everyone ran down the stairs together, and right into the arms of the uniforms who were walking up the stoop at the time."

"Okay, thanks you two, that gets me off to a decent start." Tommy replied before being interrupted by Lieutenant Bricks.

"We also have notified the Asian Gang unit and made a call to get an interpreter up here as well, don't know when either will arrive, though."

"Awesome, Lu, thanks. Alright, well I'm going to interview our Johns first, and see if we can get anything more and kick them loose."

***

Tommy removed one John at a time, from where they currently sat with a patrol officer in the muster room, just across the hall from the squad room. He took them into the interview room, which was inside of the squad room, the interview room known to the detectives as "The Box", was a small, windowless, room with a table, a couple of chairs, and a bench along the wall. There was a two-way mirror that could be looked through from an adjoining room. This is where Detective Mark Stein observed Tommy, looking for anything Tommy may miss during these interviews. In the corner was a camera, mounted where the wall met the ceiling, that faced the interviewees and recorded each interview in its entirety.

John #1 John Donner:

"Okay, Mr. Donner, by now you know why you are here. I know you have already been interviewed by my colleague, Detective Doyle, but this is my investigation and I wanted to speak to you again. In case there is anything you may have remembered or forgotten to tell Detective Doyle. I know it's late, but I'm sure you are aware we have a dead young woman whose death is a mystery to us, so we may still be awhile before we know who will be going home today, and who may not... So, without any further delay, Mr. Donner, please tell me what you witnessed this evening."

"Sure, Detective, I have nothing to hide and I'm, I'm more than happy to help you as much as I can...I, I arrived at Q's pretty close to about nine o'clock, spoke to the old guy that sits at the desk, who told me it would be a minute. Two men were leaving as I sat down on one of the chairs in the waiting area, the other two men you have here tonight were already seated, we didn't talk at all. I sat and just about as soon as my ass hit the chair this guy walks out of one of the girls' rooms and says something about his girl not trying hard enough, not being cooperative or sexy enough, and he wants his money back. The old guy is very respectful and says he will give him his money back, which surprised me to tell you the truth, but this guy was a kind of big and scary looking guy and was angry. I also thought, or got the impression, he may be a regular?"

"Why did you think that?"

"I don't know, he just had a familiar way of speaking to the old guy."

"Have you ever seen him before?"

"The big guy? No."

"But you have seen the older guy before?"

"Yes… Yes, I have visited this location twice before."

"Okay… Go ahead with what happened tonight."

"Right, well the older man went into the room and yelled at the girl, then came out and handed the big guy some money, I don't know how much. The fat woman came out from the bathroom and the old man said something to her in Chinese, then the big guy accompanied the fat woman back into the room the big guy had come from. We could all hear some yelling. We, as in us guys, sitting on the chairs waiting, then from what it sounded like, she… The fat lady started to beat the girl in the room, and then the big guy ran out of the apartment, and the fat lady quickly followed grabbing her belongings, screaming something in Chinese. The three of us just sat for a second watching all this, and as all the Chinese began to run out the door, we all hopped up and followed. None of us had a clue what had happened, none of us, we were all just sitting, and waiting, but we knew we better beat it, if the Chinese were running like the place was on fire, we knew we better get the hell out as well... And well you know the rest, those uniformed guys were waiting at the entrance of the building as we made it to the first floor and grabbed everyone, then you guys showed up, and that's it, the end."

"Okay, thank you... Now you say you have been there twice before, and you called the place Q? Is that the name of this brothel? -- Q?"

"Yes, sir, they call themselves 'The Q' as in Quality, Massage Parlor, but it's not, it's a whorehouse, and it moves every few months... I have, well, I'm a little ashamed to say, I have visited this one twice before, and gone to one of the previous locations five times before. I'm certainly not proud of it, or of myself, but it's an easy and inexpensive way to satisfy my needs."

"I'm not judging you, Mr. Donner; I'm just trying to find out what happened to this young woman?"

"Yes, sir, well I don't know and really can't tell you more... As far as if the fat lady threw her out the window or if she, if she jumped, and although I don't know the other two guys I was sitting with, I can certainly vouch for them too. We were all just sitting and waiting for the girls to come out so we could make our choices, and then everything went nuts."

"Make your choices? Please explain?"

"Well, how it works is the girls who aren't with a customer will come out, and line up, and whoever is next will pick one and then be led to the girl's room and do whatever it is you want to do and have paid for."

"And it sounds like you pay the old guy, not the girls."

"Yes, that is correct. You pay the manager who is usually, well has always been, a man whenever I have done this. The girls will sweat you for tips once you're done, but that's a rookie mistake because the girls aren't allowed to keep any of the money, at least that's what I've been told... So, tipping them is just paying extra to the house."

"You've been at least seven times now; do you know any of these girls by name?"

"Yes and no, they all have made up hooker names, Sunshine, Bunny, Happiness...shit like that, no real names."

"Okay, and do any of them speak English?"

"Oh yeah, they all do, some not very well, some surprisingly well, same with the old guy's, the managers. I know they're all playing that no English game with you right now but don't be fooled. The managers absolutely speak English, and all of the girls I have ever had, have spoken some English too, surprisingly good English...A couple I have even had short conversations with."

"Do you know any of the girls out there right now?"

"Yes, I recognize one, the girl in the purple negligee calls herself Happiness, her English is broken, but you can definitely have a conversation with her... And the old guy is Boss Lo, or just Boss, and his accent is strong but speaks plenty of English, believe me."

"What does a visit to Q, cost?"

"That can change, and can be negotiated, but you can figure for a regular visit, $80 to $100 for a blow job, $220 to $300 for sex, and for $400, you can do whatever you want, and take a trip around the world."

Tommy knew what Mr. Donner had meant but he wanted him to repeat and explain his statement for the camera. "A trip around the world? What's that?"

"Oh, uh, a trip around the world you know oral, anal, and vaginal, you can use all three holes, whatever you want."

"Okay, got it, and you said it's also negotiable?"

"Yes, yes sir, seems like different managers, and at different times of the day, or depending on how busy they are you can sometimes make a deal, and maybe get $20 to $50 dollars off."

"You seem to know a lot about this, Mr. Donner."

"To be honest, Detective, I have done this maybe a dozen times in the last two to three years, like I said, it's nothing I'm proud of, but it's easy. I was divorced several years ago, and I, well I could never connect with anyone since, and this is just an easy and inexpensive way to meet my needs… I know you probably think I am disgusting, I'm sure Detective Doyle does, but it hasn't been easy being single, and although that's no excuse, it, well I was desperate, and heard about this place and have stopped by on occasion, yes."

"Okay, Mr. Donner, we have all your information, you have no priors, and no warrants, so we are going to let you go. I may, however, be contacting you in the future with this case, now understand this… Please understand this, because we are letting you go right now, it doesn't mean nothing will come of this, but if you continue to cooperate as you have here tonight, I am fairly certain the DA's office will have no interest in coming after you in any way, once this case is closed…understand?"

"Yes, sir I do, thank you."

John #2 Avraham Krinsky

"Hello, Mr. Krinsky, I'm Detective Keane, and I know you have already given a statement to Detective Colletti, but I am here to follow up a bit."

"Hello, Detective, yes yes, ask away, I am an open book to you, I have no idea what happened to that poor woman, but I will answer whatever you ask."

"Thank you, Mr. Krinsky, now from what I understand you were waiting to pick out a prostitute to have sex with earlier this evening, sometime around nine o'clock at 439 East 80th Street, am I correct?

Avraham Krinsky hung his head low, stared into his lap for a moment, and then lifted it up making eye contact with Tommy.

"Ahhh, yes, Detective, you are correct, but only if you count the oral sex as true sex. I only receive the oral sex from these women… Never the real stuff… AIDS you know… You can't be too careful, Detective."

"Yes, Mr. Krinsky that is true. Please now tell me what you witnessed earlier this evening?"

"Not a lot. I was sitting, waiting my turn, and then a client, a client, he came out and complained to the manager about his date... And then there was some yelling, and then there was some screaming, and then the big woman went inside the room with the client in question, and there was more yelling and more screaming and then everyone ran from the apartment, and well, I thought it prudent I should run too, so I did, I ran too."

'Okay, and did any of you men sitting and waiting have any interactions with any prostitutes up to that point?"

'No, Detective, definitely not, we all just came in and sat down. I don't think anyone of us was there for more than a few minutes, one gentleman had left when I arrived, and then this dispute happened with the other gentleman, and then, then all the noise began, and we all ran out of the apartment."

"Alright, Mr. Krinsky, can you tell me who was the last person to be in the room with the woman we found on the sidewalk?"

"Yes, the older big woman, the Chinese woman, and the large man in a navy coat, they went inside, and she yelled and quite possibly there was a physical altercation, the man left first then the big woman and then we all ran out."

"Okay, Mr. Krinsky, I have all your information, you have never been arrested before I see, so we are going to let you go. I may, however, be contacting you in the future with this case, now understand this... Please, Mr. Krinsky, understand this, because we are letting you go right now, it doesn't mean nothing will come of this, but if you continue to cooperate as you have here tonight, I am fairly certain the DA's office will have no interest in coming after you in any way, once this case is closed...do you understand?"

"Yes, Detective, I understand, I understand fully and thank you."

John #3 Jacob Blake

"Hello, Mr. Blake, I am Detective Keane. I know it's been a long night for you, but it's been a long night for all of us. Detective Doyle has informed me of her interview with you earlier, and you seem to be cooperative, so I will do my best to keep this short and simple. Not to make it any easier on you, but in the hopes of getting through the next several interviews in a timely manner, so, please tell me what you can about what happened while you were visiting the brothel at 439 East 80th Street earlier."

"Hello. Detective, I've heard of you, and read about you in the newspapers. And yes, well you got me, I was indeed visiting a massage parlor tonight, but…"

Tommy interrupted; "Please, Mr. Blake, I have your previous statement, and we both know you were not looking to get yourself a massage last night, so let's not play any word games."

Tommy interrupted, and made this statement, because he immediately felt a bit of arrogance in Mr. Blake's posture and attitude, and Tommy just wanted to set the tone and remind Mr. Blake that he was in custody. That this was a serious investigation, and at this early hour, Tommy had no patience for nonsense and wanted to make sure Mr. Blake understood that.

Jacob Blake was taken aback for a moment, he took a second, and then continued; "Uh yes, Detective, you are correct,

I was not there to receive a message. I was there to have sex with a prostitute, and I had, I had arrived just moments before whatever happened, happened, and we all exited the premises."

"I arrived, and was seated against the wall, almost immediately after my arrival the Orthodox, or Hasidic man, you just spoke to arrived. He sat in the same row of chairs where I was sitting, and then the other man, the one in the flannel shirt, entered. Basically, for the most part we all arrived at the same time... Almost as soon as the man in the flannel took his seat another man, a large white male, maybe forty to fifty years old, with a dark full beard, angrily exited the room he was in and confronted the manager. He said his girl wasn't willing, or able, to satisfy him in some way, it was tense to say the least, I mean, I mean, it's fairly tense visiting a place like this to begin with, and then there was this loud verbal altercation, well, the manager didn't argue, and he gave the man his money back. He then went to yell at the girl, woman, prostitute, in the room and as he left the girl's room, this other Asian woman appeared out of nowhere... the heavyset, Asian woman you brought here with us. She immediately entered the room the manager had just left with the big bearded man, and we all could hear her screaming like a mad woman, and then what sounded like a physical fight, the man, the bearded man left the apartment altogether and then she came running out of the room, screaming in whatever dialect of Chinese these people speak, and proceeded to run out of the apartment, and the three of us waiting on the chairs followed and ran right into the police officers who were waiting at the entrance of the building for us." Blake finished with a huff, followed by a deep breath, as if he were relieved to once again get the story out.

"Okay, so again, Mr. Blake, who was the last person to see or speak to the young woman we found on the sidewalk?" Tommy asked.

"That would be the older, heavyset, Asian woman or possibly the bearded man, but I would say the older woman. She was absolutely the last person to be with that girl, or in that room with her, as he, the man left just seconds before."

"And you are certain of this?"

"Yes, absolutely certain."

"Mr. Blake, I am going to release you now, we have all your information, you have no priors, and no warrants, so we are going to let you go, we may, however, be contacting you in the future in regards this case. Now understand me, because we are letting you go right now, doesn't mean nothing else will come from this case, but if you continue to cooperate as you have so far tonight, I am pretty sure the DA's office will have no interest in you once this case is closed...do you understand me, Mr. Blake?"

"Yes, sir, I do, Detective."

***

After finishing with Jacob Blake, Tommy convened with Mark and Lieutenant Bricks. At this hour Doreen and Jimmy had signed out for the evening, leaving these three on their own.

Tommy began, "So, it looks like if this was a homicide, it's most likely to be the older Asian woman we're looking at for it, since from what we understand so far, and has been stated by all three of our witnesses, she was the last one in the room with our victim at the time. That being said, there is still this un-apprehended individual, the large, bearded man who is a possible suspect, and we still have four more interviews to do, and still no interpreter on hand… Any word from the Asian Gang Unit, Lu?"

"Nothing more than they've been notified."

"Alright, well I guess we'll have to continue then; I'm thinking we save our suspect for last, maybe interview the manager first, then each of the girls, see if we can get anything else that we can add to our questioning of our prime suspect?"

"Yeah, I think that's the way to go." Mark replied.

"Absolutely, it only makes sense, maybe we can pick up one or two new pieces we can hit her with along the way?" Lieutenant Bricks added.

They went and pulled the older man, the supposed manager, from the muster room and stuck him in the box, again as before, Tommy was alone during the interview and Stein, joined by Bricks, observed from the observation room.

Tommy began his interview of the manager, "I am Detective Keane, and I'll be asking you some questions about what happened tonight… And what is your name, sir?"

The man said nothing for a moment, then said, "Teddy."

"Okay, Teddy, how about you tell me what you can about what happened tonight?"

"No speak Engrish—Lawyer please." Was Teddy's answer.

Tommy sighed, it was now approaching 5:00 AM, and he was getting both physically and mentally tired, and he knew he had several more hours to go. He leaned back in his chair, closed his note pad, stood, and exited the interview room.

As he entered the hall, Lieutenant Bricks and Stein exited the observation room.

"He lawyered up." Tommy said flatly.

"Yeah, we saw," Bricks replied, "No English my ass, guys job is talking to English speaking Johns all day, wouldn't be surprised if he knew a few more languages as well."

"Makes no difference now, the fuckers lawyered up. I guess we'll talk to the girls next, I doubt any of them will be forthcoming. I'm sure they're all terrified of us, and ten times as afraid of what will happen to them if they talk, but we'll see, maybe one of them will make a mistake and give us a little something? Give me a minute, I need to take a break, you wanna stick this guy in a cell and I'll be right back for whatever girl you have ready, Mark?"

"Yeah, go ahead Tom, take your time."

***

Tommy put on his jacket and went downstairs and out onto the street. He checked his phone, it was 05:08 AM, he took a deep breath of the cold January air and leaned against a patrol car that was parked outside the precinct. As he did, he saw the silhouettes of a man and a woman walking down the block, as they approached, he could see they were both Asian.

The man stood about five foot six inches tall and wore a long, tan, camel hair coat, and a grey scally cap with ear flaps that were pulled down over his ears. The woman appeared to be no more than about five feet tall, maybe five one if that. She was wearing a long, black, wool coat, and had her long jet-black hair done up in a tall pompadour in the front, possibly in an attempt to make her appear taller than her very slight stature would permit?

As they turned and stepped onto the steps of the precincts stoop, Tommy pushed himself off the car and asked out loud from behind, "You two from the gang unit?"

The couple stopped and turned, then simultaneously answered, "Yes."

"Detective John Hua." The man said.

"And I am Detective Yan, Lisa Yan. We are from the Asian gang unit."

"Nice to meet yous, I'm Detective Keane, you're here for my case, come on, let's go inside out of the cold and I'll tell you what we got."

Tommy led Detectives Hua, and Yan, up to the squad room on the second floor and as he did, he gave them a synopsis of the evening's events and where they had gotten, as far as the interviews and investigation, over the last eight hours.

They entered the squad room and Tommy introduced Hua and Yan to Lieutenant Bricks and Stein, then took down their names and shield numbers for his unusual incident report.

"I'm actually surprised to meet you two tonight." Tommy began, "I was just expecting a phone call confirming you had been notified, and maybe a question or two. You guys certainly don't go out on house calls every time a notification comes through, do you?"

"Ahh, no," Detective Yan began with a smile, "You see I got the message from your colleague, a, a Detective Doyle, and the description she gave, the description she gave of the very heavy woman piqued my interest. You see, Detective Keane, I think, we think, and no joke or pun intended, you may have landed yourself a whale here."

"What's that?" Lieutenant Bricks asked.

"We think the woman you have in custody may be Mama Woo, Lieutenant."

"I'm sorry I'm not familiar, Detective." Lieutenant Bricks replied.

"Nor am I," said Tommy.

"She, well if it is indeed her… May be Mama Woo, who is one of the leaders of probably the most notorious and vicious Chinese gangs in the country." Hua said.

"Really?" Tommy asked, "Please fill us in."

"Yeah, tell us who this Mama Woo is, we'd like to know who we have in custody." Asked Lieutenant Bricks.

"Well, Lu, Detectives, I'll let Lisa fill you in, she is really the expert on everything Woo related, go ahead Lisa."

"Thanks, John." Lisa replied.

***

Li Jun

Lisa Yan was born and raised on Bayard Street in Manhattan's Chinatown. She graduated from The Bronx High School of Science, "Bronx Science", and later graduated from RIT, The Rochester Institute of Technology with a Bachelors in biochemistry. She then immediately proceeded to disappoint her family by entering the New York City Police Academy approximately eight months after said graduation.

Lisa Yan couldn't help herself. To her, police work was a calling, she felt it was a career she had to pursue, it was something she grew up dreaming about as a young girl. As it happened though, the job 'Police Officer', turned out to be incredibly demanding, and one that Lisa Yan, who stood only five-foot one inch tall, weighed only one hundred and fourteen pounds, and spoke with the voice of a young, grade-school girl was most definitely not cut out for.

And although first assigned to the relatively quiet 107th Precinct in Queens, the young Officer Lisa Yan, found policing to be a relatively impossible job. The complete lack of respect she received from the public, as well as by her fellow officers due to her diminutive stature and soft spoken rather mousey personality, was completely disheartening and demoralizing.

Where Lisa eventually found her niche was in the fact that she spoke not only fluent Mandarin, but was fluent in six other Chinese dialects, and had studied Russian and Polish, while at RIT. She also had a good grasp of German as well. By her third year on the job, PO Lisa Yan was flying all over the city as a translator, to assist in all sorts of cases, in every corner, of every borough, of the city.

It was during this time that she, as well as her superiors, realized just what an asset she was to the department, and once assigned to Detective Bureau Queens, she was able to make a name for herself. As it would turn out, everything Police Officer Lisa Yan was missing, and needed to be a good patrol officer, was not nearly as important as what she could offer the department as a whole, and what made her in the end, a brilliant investigator.

No doubt it was her linguistic abilities that opened the door for Lisa, but it was her attention to detail, and her ability to focus on, and tenaciously follow, her instincts that made her a truly great investigator. Much like Tommy, Lisa had a calling and a talent. Sure, she wasn't chasing drug dealers across rooftops, and there were no stories about kicking down doors, wild beatdowns, or deadly shootouts: but make no mistake, if your name came up in a Lisa Yan case folder, you were going to get got. Lisa, as small and diminutive as she was, had game.

***

"Well, if this is indeed Mama Woo," Lisa began. "She and her older brother, Peter Woo, are leaders of the Purple Dragon Gang. They operate all over the city, and have affiliate chapters in San Francisco, Toronto, and possibly Montreal, as well. Although in their early forties, their gang... Their organization I should say, is relatively young, in comparison to the traditional Chinese organized crime Tongs you may be familiar with. They are newcomers, they deal in both human and drug trafficking, they are completely ruthless individuals, and are hated by the larger old school Tongs here in New York and California."

Tommy asked, "The Purple Dragons? Isn't that…"

"Yes, ironically it is the gang's name from the Ninja Turtles, believe me, there is no connection." Detective Hua interjected then Lisa Yan continued.

"You may remember several years ago, there was a small war in Chinatown here in the city, rumors are the killings were between the Woo's, Purple Dragon Gang and the Ha Sing Tong, who have been in Chinatown for over a hundred years. There were almost a dozen homicides in a three-month period that summer, and they were quite brutal."

"I remember," Stein interrupted, "They were mutilating, and hanging, each other's bodies from fire escapes."

"Yes, well, that was the Woo's and the Dragons, the old time Tongs will kill, but the Purple Dragons, were making extreme examples of their victims, and this was bad, really bad for business in Chinatown. So, the old guard made a truce and a deal with the Woo's, the violence ended in Chinatown, and everyone went back to making money.

"If this is Mama Woo, and if you do indeed have her for a homicide, this is big, Detective Keane."

"Tommy, please call me Tommy."

"We've been tracking her and her brother for years, the FBI has folders on them and their associates also, as well as Immigration and the ATF… Now again, you think she has thrown a sex worker out of a window, is that what you're going to charge her with?"

"We haven't completed our interviews, and I haven't reached out to the DA's office yet, but it certainly looks that way at the moment. She appears to be the madame of this brothel over here on 80th Street, she was the last to be in the room with the victim during a heated argument, the young woman goes out the window to her death, and the old fat woman she was arguing with has scratches on her wrist. No eyewitness, and the witnesses we spoke to don't understand Chinese. The brothel manager lawyered up just before your arrival, and we have three prostitutes left to question… That, Detective, is where we are at."

"Please, Tommy, call me Lisa."

"You want to meet our Madame?"

"Absolutely, but let us take a look at her first, I'd like to see if she is indeed Mama Woo. I only know her from photographs, John too, we've never seen her in the flesh."

"Never? I thought you'd been tracking them for years?"

"Yes, but she is amazingly elusive, both her and Peter Woo, avoid public events and appearances. We have no idea where they even live. We do know they have several properties held in shell companies here in the City, in Brooklyn, Queens, and New Jersey."

"How do they do business and not be seen?"

"Through their underlings. They have soldiers in the organization who do everything. The Purple Dragons street operations are run by a pair of twin brothers, Marty and Tony Chu, we know they are responsible for carrying out all sorts of crimes for the Woo's. They are the equivalent to Capo's in the

Italian mob, they run all the street business, and pay up to the Woos, who use their international and political connections to keep the product coming in from China. But even *they* are impossible to catch in the act, they delegate and enforce within the Purple Dragons, and sadly the victims of the street soldiers never make complaints to the police. Forget about testifying after an arrest – it's all so internal, it's all kept within the community, you see, and with few to no complaints coming in, and a silent community, we, well we have so little to build cases on outside of the street gangs."

"It's true, the silence from the community and distrust of the police in general, make our investigations into these gangs, and particularly the Woos, very very difficult, nearly impossible." Detective Hua added.

"So, you wanna take a look?" Tommy asked.

Chapter Five

Tommy, Stein, and Lieutenant Bricks led Detectives Yan, and Hua, to the muster room. They stopped at the door and looked through its wired safety glass window.

"Look, John," Lisa whispered excitedly, "Look, it's her!"

"Fuck me – it is." Was his simple four-word reply.

John and Lisa paused and stared through the window for a moment. Peter and Mama Woo had been under the Asian Gang Units scrutiny for as long as either of these detectives had been attached to it, but neither of them had ever seen these notorious siblings in the flesh. Occasionally, you'd get a glimpse in a photograph, or some grainy video, but here she was, seated on a blue plastic chair, her arms folded and her head back against the wall, napping.

Their eyes scanned the room. A uniform officer sat in a chair near the door. The woman now confirmed to be Mama Woo, sat against the far wall, almost directly across from the window the detectives were looking through. About eight to ten feet from her sat Teddy, the manager, then each of the younger sex workers, the second lying on the floor with her eyes closed, all of them separated by eight to ten feet, and all of them trying to get some sleep.

"Do you recognize anyone else?" Lieutenant Bricks asked.

"I don't, – Lisa?" John Hua answered and asked.

"No, no, Lieutenant I don't. Obviously, the man is the one you referred to as the manager, and the other three are obviously sex workers, and you say you haven't interviewed any of them yet, right?" Lisa replied.

"We spoke to the manager, but he lawyered up right away, said 'No English—Lawyer' then repeated that once or twice." Tommy said.

"Yeah, that's a shame, hmm… how would you like to proceed, Detective Keane?" Lisa asked.

"Well, what do you guys think? We were going to pull each of the girls next and see if we could get anything out of them, then interview Mama Woo. Do you guys want to conduct the interview with Keane so they can't pull the no English shit?" Lieutenant Bricks asked.

"What do you say, Lisa, John? I bring each girl in individually, speak with them while you observe, then speak to you and maybe have you step in, Lisa, especially if there is a language problem, I, I assume you speak Chinese, yes?" Tommy asked, unaware if his assumption could possibly be frowned upon.

"Ha ha," John Hua laughed, "Yes, we both speak Chinese, but this one – she can speak six different dialects, along with Russian, German, and Polish too. I can only speak the Standard Chinese, what we call Beijing Mandarin, but this one is, well she is wow, when it comes to languages."

"Really? That is impressive, Detective." Lieutenant Bricks replied.

"Detective Hua exaggerates, I am currently learning German, and am far from fluent." Lisa said sheepishly, as she was somehow embarrassed by her linguistic abilities. "But yes, Tommy, I think that is a good approach. We will observe from the observation room, then follow up once you are finished, assuming we can get anywhere with any of them. To be honest, I don't think they are going to say anything, but I think I'd rather watch from the observation room, maybe they'll slip up and say something stupid in Chinese, and we'll be able to pick it up, something they wouldn't ordinarily say if they knew anyone would understand them."

"I like it, okay, I'll interview them alone, and you four watch and listen, see if we get anything. I'll also play dumb, with Mama Woo, and won't let her know we have any idea who she is, first I'll go easy, then maybe take a break and return harder and threaten her with the homicide charges, sound good?"

"Sounds like a plan, good luck cracking this egg, Detective." Lisa answered.

***

Tommy brought the first of the three sex workers into the interview room.

"Please sit. Are you thirsty? Would you like something to eat or drink?"

The young woman looked down at the table and shook her head no.

"Okay, I am Detective Keane, I'm going to ask you about what happened tonight, at 439 East 80th Street, please take your time. Know I am not here to harm you at all or in anyway, we are on your side and are only looking for the truth dear, do you understand me? How is your English? Do you understand what I am saying?"

The young woman nodded yes.

"Okay, very good, what is your name, Miss?

Never removing her eyes from the table, she softly answered in a heavy Chinese accent.

"Violet."

"Okay, Violet, what can you tell me about tonight, and what happened at 439?"

The young woman continued to stare at the table and nodded no.

"Come on, you can tell me something, Violet, what happened tonight?"

Again, she shook her head no, then spoke softly, "Nothing."

"Violet... C'mon, now, you know why we are here, and you saw what happened to your friend, you have to know something, now what can you tell me?"

She again shook her head, "I know nothing, nothing."

"Who is the older large woman that was brought in with you?"

"I don't know her."

"Look at me dear," Tommy asked and leaned into the table to get a little closer to Violet, "Please help me, did the large woman and the girl who went out the window have a fight?"

Violet continued to stare at the table, "I don't know."

"Who is Teddy to you?"

"I don't know him?"

"What were you doing in the apartment at 439?"

"I don't know."

This went on for several more questions, Tommy quickly tiring of it, excused himself and went back to the observation room.

"You saw – nothing. You want to take a crack at her?"

"I don't expect much but I will try," Lisa said, "Come sit with me, I will try to help explain you are one of the good guys and trying to help."

Tommy and Lisa reentered the interview room, Lisa introduced herself, this time speaking in Mandarin, she explained what was going on, who Tommy was, and why they were all here in the interview room. She then proceeded, again in Mandarin, to ask many of the same questions Tommy asked, and to each question asked, received the same reply. "I know nothing, I don't know her, I don't know him, I don't know why I was there."

She knew nothing about nothing, never took her eyes from the table, showed little emotion at all until Detective Lisa Yan asked young Violet who the victim on the street was and if she knew her name?

"Harmony," Violet said it plainly and clearly, "Harmony."

"Do you know her real name?" Lisa asked in Mandarin.

"Li – Harmony, is Li."

"What can you tell me about Li, Violet?"

"I know nothing."

This went on for several more questions, until Lisa tired of asking them, and Violet was removed from the interview room.

***

The next young woman was brought in, and Tommy began to introduce himself, "Hello, my name is Detec…"

"I no say nothing to you!" This one spoke up immediately, fearlessly, and defiantly, "Nothing to you! Nothing!"

"Wow, is that how you really want to start this interview? I was going to offer you something to drink and some food, you must be hungry and a little thir…" again he was cut off.

"I no say nothing to you!" She yelled again.

Lisa left the observation room and knocked on the door as she let herself in, she began speaking in Mandarin to the young woman.

"Fuck you, bitch, I say nothing, nothing!" The woman answered aggressively in English.

Lisa tried again but couldn't get three words out of her mouth before she was again interrupted with profanities, first in English, then in Mandarin.

She looked over at Tommy, "I don't think she is going to say anything, Detective."

***

The final sex worker left was brought into the interview room, Tommy again introduced himself, and asked her if she would like something to eat or drink, she shook her head no.

"Can you tell us about what happened tonight at 439 East 80th Street?"

The young woman shook her head no, and like the first, stared down at the table in front of her.

"Can you... Will you tell me something, anything about Harmony? Was she? Was Harmony, was Li, your friend?"

The young woman nodded her head yes.

"Please, can you tell me more?"

"Li was my friend." She said softly with a heavy accent.

"I'm sorry, I'm so sorry dear, I know it must hurt to lose her." Tommy said in as comforting a tone as he could muster. "What can you tell me about Li?"

The young woman sat silently for a few seconds.

"Please, I want to help, I want to punish whoever did this to her."

A tear rolled from the young woman's eye. "Li was my friend, my only friend in whole world, my best friend, we, she, like a sister, and, and I love her."

"Please, dear," looking down at his notes to recall her name, "Sunshine, I need you Sunshine, I know nothing, and I can't help unless I know everything."

She looked up at him, tiny, frail, tears running down her cheeks. "They will torture and kill me—but I will tell you, I will tell you all I know—Li Jun was my only friend in this world."

"Thank you, Sunshine, may I ask dear, what is your real name?"

"I, I am—Min, they name me Sunshine, I am Min, they name Li, Harmony, she is Li."

And with that she began. Min's English was broken but overall, very good, and Tommy didn't interrupt her at all as she told him how she had met Li when she was eleven. Her mother handed her off to a man in China, who was to take her in to be trained and schooled on how to work in the hotel business in America, she was put into a small van with six or seven other girls, one of which was Li.

They almost immediately bonded, a few days later they and several other girls and two young boys, who were picked up along the way, arrived in a large unknown city. Upon arrival, they were placed in a small apartment, and were introduced to two men and two women, who ran this particular apartment. These four were much less friendly than the man Min's and Li's parents had introduced them to, and once in the apartment it was very apparent their lives had forever changed.

These children had indeed arrived in a school of sorts. Here the twelve children were almost immediately all beaten, and then individually raped. During the rapes and beatings, they were instructed not to cry or to complain. It was explained, and re-explained, to them that they were now officially the property of the masters of the house, and sex was now how they were to earn a living and survive.

Min explained in detail how terrified she and the other children were, and how she could not believe her mother had sent her to live with these people. It was here that Min and Li's bond began to grow strong, as the only comfort either had was with one another.

After about a week, their group was slowly broken up, two or three children leaving with one man, two to four with another. Min and Li were with a group of four girls who left with two men about ten days after arriving at the apartment.

They were moved to another unknown apartment where they were fed well, and for the most part left alone, for several days until one morning where they were taken to a large ship which was loaded with hundreds of other Chinese people of every age. Here a strong, young man watched over and protected them for several days until they arrived in the country of Canada.

In Canada, they were moved to two apartments, where they stayed with several other children and teenage girls, none of whom had any idea what was going on in their lives, but all shared the almost identical experience as Min and Li, and all of whom now lived in complete terror of what the next day would bring.

Early one morning, Min explained, a dozen of them, all girls, were loaded into a white passenger van with Church of Lord written in English and Chinese on the side of it. They were driven into Washington, of the United States, and then days later put on an airplane and brought to New York.

Here in New York, they were introduced to Mama Woo, who made it very clear that they were all her property, and that they would have to work for her for many years to earn their freedom.

Mama Woo was a very intimidating woman. She was very mean and very harsh. Speaking out of turn, or a cross look, was immediately met with a slap or a blow with a closed fist. On the day of their first meeting, Min stated one of the older girls who was about fourteen, was burned with a cigarette in front of all of the others for no reason whatsoever, other than to show what would happen if anyone got out of line.

As Min went on with her story, she began to visibly relax with Tommy, she even began to raise her voice slightly as she became more confident. She continued to cry, and occasionally had to stop for a deep breath, but it was apparent to Tommy, as well as the others in the observation room, that they had a cooperative witness who may have a lot of evidence to share with the squad.

Min continued for some time and explained how for the last seven to eight years she and Li were sex slaves, who worked as prostitutes for the Woo gang, seven days a week, servicing anywhere from ten to as many as twenty-five clients a day.

Finally, Tommy asked, "Is that Mama Woo outside?"

Min looked down, pursed her lips, and nodded her head, "Yes, she Mama Woo."

Tommy then leaned in and softly asked, "Did Mama Woo kill Li?"

Min looked up at Tommy, "I say yes."

"Please dear, what do you know—what can you tell me?"

"I know client complain, he complain Li not sexy enough, Li not try hard enough to love client good enough, he demand money back, and Mama Woo get angry and go to Li's room. I hear yelling, slapping, hitting, then Mama Woo run out and tell to Teddy in Chinese "Get out! Get out! She gone! Li gone now! Out! Out! —She crazy, Mama Woo, she panicked, and screaming at us all to get out... Then I see when we leave building, I see, I see why, I see what Mama Woo do."

Min then broke down and began to cry and rock in her seat. Tommy and the other detectives had just listened to her horrid life story, right up to the death of her only friend, a young 19-year-old named Li, who was now only referred to as Harmony, and who until her violent end, just hours ago, also only had one friend in the entire world, this sad little 19-year-old woman Min, who's only reason for living was now gone.

Tommy reached across the table and placed his hand on Min's shoulder, then stood up and walked around the table and knelt on one knee beside her, putting one arm around her and gently pulling her close he said very softly, "I will keep you safe

Min, I promise we will not let the Woos hurt you, and I will make sure they pay for what they've done to you, and Li, and the others. I will do everything I can, Min, everything."

Tommy knelt for a minute longer. Now speechless, he let Min cry. She eventually took a deep breath, then nodded yes, in acknowledgment to what Tommy had said.

Tommy then stood up, still with one hand on Min's shoulder, "Min, I have work to do now, I'm going to leave you here in this room, okay, you are safe here, and I will keep you safe. You will not be going back in the other room with Mama Woo, and the others, okay, stay here. I will get you a blanket and some clothes, try and relax dear, and please know, that I am on your side, okay."

Min looked up into Tommy's eyes, she lifted her hand up and placed it on top of the one Tommy had on her shoulder. Not since she was eleven had she ever had one ounce of trust for a man, literally everyone she had ever met, had used and abused her. But, somehow in these last few moments she believed Tommy just may be her savior. As she continued to look up into his eyes, she nodded yes, and gently tightened the hand she had placed atop his.

Tommy gently tightened his hand on her shoulder in response, then left the room. He stopped just outside the door, once it closed, he had to pause and take a deep breath. Although he was able to keep his composure throughout the interview, what Min had told him, although no surprise, shattered him, and for the sake of professionalism, he needed to pause before speaking to Lieutenant Bricks, Stein, and the others.

As he inhaled deeply, the door to the observation room opened and Lieutenant Bricks stepped out, Tommy raised his hand with his index finger extended to say one minute. Lieutenant Bricks, immediately recognized the look on Tommy's face and stepped back inside, placing his hand on Detective Hua's chest, and softly saying, "Step back in for a moment, please."

Li Jun

Chapter Six

Detectives Stein, Yan, and Hua, along with Lieutenant Bricks, all stayed in the observation room. Tommy regained his composure, then removed Min from the interview room and walked her to Lieutenant Bricks office. Then had a uniformed officer join her, he waited a moment for them to get situated, then went and woke up Mama Woo and walked her to the interview room. He directed her to sit at a table in a chair against the wall on the far side of the room.

Tommy began, and hiding his disdain, calmly began to interview her, "Hello Miss, I'm Detective Keane, and I want to ask you some questions about what happened tonight at 439 East 80th Street, the building where you were met and taken into custody by the uniformed officers, may I ask you ma'am, are you understanding me fully?

Mama Woo nodded in affirmation.

"You do, so your English is good then, and you fully understand what I'm saying, yes?"

"My English is excellent, Detective Keane, and yes, I understand everything you are saying." Mama Woo replied in perfect English, although with a discernible Chinese accent.

"Okay great, we're off to a good start then. I want to know what you can tell me about tonight, and what happened at the apartment, let's start with…" Tommy paused as Mama Woo raised one finger in a gesture for him to do so.

"Yes ma'am?" Tommy asked.

"Do you find my English to be good, Detective? I take pride in my English, and in my French, I have taken many lessons in both."

"Yes, ma'am, I find your English to be very good, and I…" again Tommy stopped as Mama Woo, slowly raised her finger.

"Oh, so very good, I do have important thing to tell you, Detective, and I want to make sure you understand me, and my English through my accent." She paused for effect.

"Yes, and what is that, Miss?"

"My. Lawyer. Please." She said flatly, with zero expression on her face, and crossing her arms in front of her, as she finished those three little words.

Tommy leaned back in his chair and stared at her for a moment, then took a deep breath and stood and left the room. He headed over to the observation room and entered.

"Exactly what we expected." Hua stated as Tommy closed the door.

"Yeah, she's a pro, I knew this would go nowhere." Lisa added.

Lieutenant Bricks interjected, he spoke softly but firmly, and it was apparent he was losing his patience with Woo, and her manager. "We've interviewed the prostitutes, and the Johns, I'm satisfied, book Ms. Woo, here for compelling and promoting prostitution, when you get with the ADA, you let them know there is a homicide investigation pending with this case and our Ms. Woo, is the prime suspect."

"Yes sir, you got it, Lu." Tommy answered.

***

Tommy, Stein, Lieutenant Bricks, and Detectives Hua, and Yan, all sat in a circle in the squad room, some in chairs, others on desks.

Lisa Yan spoke up as she leaned back on her hands, resting against a desk with her legs crossed at the ankles, "You got her—for years the Woos have terrorized people all over the tri-state area, and like phantoms, just vaporized into the mist of their own underworlds. Fuck yeah, we have been following her for years, only having a few known photographs of both her and her brother, and now here she is, in the room next door. We have a compelling statement, evidence that she has committed murder, promoted prostitution, and trafficked children and adults. My god my god my god, we have her, finally we have her!"

"And you're good with everything we got so far, Lu, the trafficking, and we like her for the murder, yes?"

"Fuck yeah, we do, Tommy." He replied, in a rather serious tone, knowing how exhausted Tommy was, that he was still hurting from the interview, and that he would have to go through a lot more before this case was over.

Li Jun

Chapter Seven

At approximately 9:43 AM, Tommy, Mark Stein, Lisa Yan, and John Hua were all still working on and discussing the case. A couple of members of A Squad were now also in the squad room and working on their respective cases, when two individuals stepped into the office. They were Michelle Kai and William Conroy, from the F.B.I.

"Hello, Agents Kai and Conroy here, from the FBI We're hoping to speak with a Detective Thomas Keane, if he is still here?" Agent Kai asked.

Everyone in the room looked up, and before Tommy answered, he noticed a look of disappointment come over the face of Detective Lisa Yan. He may have been wrong, and it may have been nothing, but he did notice and take a mental note of it.

"I'm Keane, what can I do for you?" Tommy said as he stood and walked across the small, cramped and now crowded squad room, shaking both Agent Kai's and Conroy's hands.

"Hello, Detective Keane, I'm very happy to meet you. I have heard of you several times and read about you as well, most recently with that child cult case, nice work Detective, it's truly an honor meeting you, sir." Agent Kai stated with a broad smile.

Tommy smiled at her and took notice of just how attractive this woman was as she complemented him.

Michelle Kai had a very nice face and smile. She wore her jet-black hair feathered back on the sides, in an almost 70's retro style reminiscent of Farah Fawcett from the old television program Charlies Angels, and it worked very well for her. She was dressed in a well-tailored, navy pin-stripe suit, and very tall black high-heeled pumps.

Her partner, William Conroy, looked more like your typical federal agent. He was about forty-five with a receding hairline. He wore a navy blazer, with a blue shirt, striped tie and khaki pants, and he seemed quite content to allow his partner, Agent Kai, do most of the talking.

"We're here because we know, or understand, that you may have arrested a woman known to the bureau as Mama Woo, are we correct, Detective? Do you indeed have Mama Woo in custody?"

"Yes, ma'am, we do."

"Really, that is fantastic, Detective Keane. She and her brother have been on our radar for several years, and we currently have several investigations going involving them both concerning a multitude of federal offenses, what – so I'm clear, have you charged her with today?"

"We've arrested Ms. Woo for a homicide, as well as kidnapping, promoting prostitution, and several other charges we'll be adding along the way."

"Homicide? A murder? Wow, and you have her, cold, no doubt?"

"Absolutely, no doubt."

"What can you share with me, Detective? May I look at your folder? Take some notes? I'd really like to see if we can work with you on this, maybe fold it into our investigation of the Woos?"

Tommy paused for a moment, "To be honest, Agent Kai, I've been up for over twenty-four hours, and have been working this case for over sixteen of those. I have a lot of stuff yet to do, and I need to get downtown and meet with the ADA who will be handling this. So really, right now, at this moment, I'm going to have to tell you no. I understand you want to get as much information as you can, to help enhance whatever you're working on with the Woo gang, but I really need to get through the rest of this shift, which won't be ending anytime soon. I really do hate to put you off right now, but I have to say no, not until I've gotten everything signed off on and handed over to the District Attorney's office."

Agent Kai now paused, she was a little taken back in how quickly Tommy had said no, it was something she wasn't accustomed to, "Detective, you do realize an FBI investigation does take precedence over a municipal investigation, do you not?"

"No, not where a homicide is concerned, Agent Kai."

She paused again for a second and looked to her partner Agent Conroy.

"He's right, Michelle." Conroy stated, and she knew he was. She was just hoping to learn as much as she could about what Tommy had found out about the elusive criminal mastermind Mama Woo.

"Can you share anything with us, Detective? We did make the trip up here this morning."

"Nothing more than you already know, Agent Kai, here's my card. By tomorrow an ADA will be assigned, and neck deep in this case. I'll let you know who it is, you can get with them on what info they'd like to share."

Michelle Kai, visibly unhappy, looked down at the card, then looked over at Lisa Yan. "Hello, Lisa."

"Michelle." Lisa replied.

Then looking back at Tommy, "Very well then, Detective Keane, you'll be hearing from us later today, or tomorrow then. Thank you very much for your time." She put her hand out, Tommy shook it and replied, "Tomorrow please, I'm looking to catch a couple of hours sleep once I leave the DA's office."

Michelle Kai nodded, and Tommy reached out for Agent Conroy's hand and remarked, "Thanks for stopping in, nice talking to you."

Conroy nodded and smiled and then both agents left the squad room.

***

"So, you and Agent Kai know one another, Lisa?"

"Yes, we've worked cases together." Lisa said emotionless.

Tommy didn't ask more; he could tell Lisa didn't care for Michelle Kai. John Hua, on the other hand, after sitting silently during the FBI's brief visit, spoke right up.

"Nah, Lisa and Michelle are less than friends. FBI have stepped all over a couple of our cases in the past, they love to have Lisa do all the language work, then take credit for the investigations, especially Michelle Kai. She likes to insert herself into someone else's work, then strut around in her designer clothes, and flip her hair around like some runway model, when it's some other Agent or Detective doing all of the heavy lifting. Thinks she's some fuckin spokesmodel for the FBI, I gotta say, she does give impressive presentations, and looks great on TV, even if she doesn't do any of the leg work."

Tommy smirked, "Well, there's nothing here for the FBI anyway, and really, there's not much of an investigation left – No mystery to be solved here – we have a dead body, a very probable perpetrator, come the autopsy, I expect to have some DNA corroboration from the Medical Examiner's office, which, fuck me, I need to get to in a couple hours. I have a witness, which I'm going to have to find lodging for. Christ, I have a lot to do still to end this day, but like I said, there's no mystery here, just a bunch of t's I gotta cross and i's I gotta dot."

***

Tommy, with the assistance of Mark Stein, and a little case enhancement by Detectives Yan and Hua, finished up the case folders for Mama Woo, Teddy, and the others.

Tommy briefly spoke with ADA Michael Bradly who had been assigned the case. He informed Bradly that he was going to head down to the autopsy and asked him if he would like to join him. They could discuss the case and he could witness the autopsy, interview the Medical Examiner himself, and if, in the meantime, he could secure lodging for their witness, Min.

Bradly agreed to it all, it was unusual to lodge a witness so early in a case, but knowing the gravity this case may hold, ADA Bradly, within an hour had a room at a midtown hotel arranged for Min, and a 1:30 time set to meet at the morgue.

***

1:26 PM

Tommy arrived at the morgue alone. Stein had headed home after lodging Min, and the rest of B Squad wouldn't be back at work until later that evening.

Tommy entered the front door and seeing no ADA waiting for him, stepped back outside where the cold air helped keep him awake. After about three minutes a cab pulled up, and a young man in a suit and tie stepped out of it. It was Michael Bradly, and from his wavy hair, horn rimmed glasses, and ill-fitting suit, he had ADA written all over him.

"ADA Bradly?" Tommy asked.

"Yes sir. Detective Keane?"

"Yes sir."

The two exchanged pleasantries, and Tommy filled him in on everything that they had so far on the case, which really wasn't a lot, as Tommy had said previously in the squad room, "There's no mystery here."

They then entered the morgue, identified themselves at the reception desk, and asked for ME. Smyth.

Smyth immediately came and got them, and as she walked them back to where the body was located, she began; "Glad you gentlemen showed up a little early, I just finished up a little while ago. Okay, so, cause of death was obvious, right? Young lady fell from third story window, impaling herself on the iron fencing below, I would guess if the fall didn't immediately kill her which I believe it did, then she was most likely unconscious after making impact with the iron fence, and was probably dead withing two minutes. Now all of this is fairly obvious, and what you two are going to want to know is what I was able to find linking her to a possible assailant, yes?"

Before either Tommy or ADA Bradly could answer, ME. Smyth continued.

"Yes, we found skin under our victim's fingernails. Now we don't have the results back, but what I am hoping is that the DNA will be a match to one of the people you have in custody and the DNA taken from the skin under your assailant's nails, will be a match to our victim here. I assume you took DNA samples from your suspect and forwarded it to the lab, Detective?"

"Yes, we took oral swabs as well as fingernail swabs to test against our victim's scratches, I also have a hair sample."

"Excellent," Smyth paused but again just long enough for a breath, and not long enough for anyone to ask any questions. All three were now around the body of young Li Jun which lay naked on a stainless-steel examining table.

"What else will you be interested to know? Well, you can see there are many smaller marks and bruises all over her body, none really severe, and many are older, but these here," pointing to Li's neck, "These happened seconds to minutes before your victim's death. I believe she was grabbed by the neck by a left hand, pushed forcefully, and squeezed hard enough to cause these bruises, same here on her upper left arm, this bruising was very close to time of death, as were these two scratches. I am going to assume, although I still have some testing to do, that our attacker grabbed her by the throat with their left hand, and by the left arm with their right and then shoved her forcefully, causing this bruising and these scratches. These marks here, around her eyes and cheeks, were from being struck repeatedly, probably with an open hand and I believe from someone wearing more than one ring."

"Yes, our suspect was wearing rings, and we have them headed to the lab as well," then turning his attention to ADA Bradly, "You alright?" Tommy asked noticing he was obviously disturbed by the body.

"Yeah, fine." Was his answer, though he visibly wasn't.

"As I told you at the scene, Detective Keane, your victim here has many scars, both old and new, consistent with being tortured. You see where she has been burnt many times with cigarettes, in between her toes, and here behind her ears at the hairline. Now this is for you to determine, but I believe these scars are from her pimps punishing her, but not wanting any of this to be visible. She has signs of a lot of recent sex, vaginal, anal, and oral, and there is also a large number of amphetamines in her system. I'll have a full report for you in a few hours, do either of you gentleman have any questions?"

"How long for the DNA to come back?" Tommy asked.

"Best case, six weeks if you're lucky, could be sixteen if you're not."

"Thanks, Smyth, overall, I think I'm good, really, you've just confirmed all I had already thought. How about you, Mike? You good?"

"Yeah, if you're satisfied, Detective, then I am."

They all shook hands, and Tommy and ADA Bradly, exited the building.

Mike Bradly quickly made his way to the curb, and placed his hand on a parked car, he wretched one time but then took a deep breath and was able to compose himself.

"Sorry Detective, I don't think I was prepared for that."

"It's okay pal, I wish I wasn't."

***

Tommy and Mike Bradly returned to the ADA's office where they swore out the complaints for the murder of Li Jun.

Tommy then called into the squad and had Charice sign him out and he headed straight to his mother's place on 88th Street.

Except for the hour-long nap, he had taken with JoJo the prior afternoon, Tommy had been up for almost thirty-six hours at this point. This was not something unusual, like every other cop and detective in the city, once you're involved in a case it can easily be tens of hours before you can take a break, and in this case the number was thirty-six. Tommy walked in the door, found his mother in her chair smoking a cigarette in front of the

TV, unaware of what she said to him, he simply replied, "I love you too, Ma, I have to get some sleep." And then went to his room and did just that.

Chapter Eight

Tommy's eyes opened, in the darkness of his room, at his mother's apartment. It was 3:36 AM, he had gotten several hours of solid sleep, and felt like a new man. He had hours until he had to make his way into the precinct, but as good as he felt, he wanted to get up and get started with the day.

Tommy rolled onto the floor and did his fifty pushups; they were a little creaky and stiffer than they usually were. After his exceptionally long day, and over ten hours in bed, he was understandably stiff. He stood up in the dark, did a little stretching, then made his way to the bathroom for a shower and a shave. After exiting the bathroom, he cracked the door to his mother's room open, and little JoJo came out shaking his little body with joy at the site of Tommy.

Tommy dressed, with JoJo by his side, then took him for a walk. Together, they made their way down to 80th Street and to the crime scene where they stood outside of the building, on this dark cold February morning. There was nothing more he really needed from this scene, he had his killer in custody, he had a witness, and now it was just a matter of weeks until the DNA would return from the lab and help to corroborate everything they knew about this case.

No, Tommy didn't need to revisit the crime scene, but something, a sadness for the victim, pulled him there, maybe he needed to pay some respect to Li?

The thought that she had no one on her side for her entire life but for one other young victim, Min, ate at Tommy a bit. Over the years, he had seen so many horrific crimes committed, and the ghosts of so many victims seemed to take up permanent residence in Tommy's memories. But this young Li, this poor young Li, who was the same age as his daughter Caitlin, studying up in Siena College, who had every opportunity her parents could offer her. In contrast, Li, had never had a single opportunity for happiness in her short, awful life.

"Nothing." Tommy said aloud, looking at the wrought iron fence that just hours ago young Li Jun, was impaled on, "Nothing, nothing but misery you poor, sweet, innocent little dear." Tommy wiped a tear from his eye, then another that ran down his other cheek.

He was hurt for this girl. He had hurt for many others in the past and he was all too familiar with the feeling, as well as the guilt. The guilt they call 'survivors' guilt', a pain, and a shame, that eats away at a person's soul when they live through a traumatic, possibly life-threatening event and come out of it unscathed, while witnessing others suffer.

No, there was nothing new to these feelings, he was well accustomed to them. As he stood in front of 439 East 80th Street, he looked up at the frieze of Minerva that stared down at the scene, "Look at me… Just two mornings ago I was feeling sorry for myself, feeling lonely, fucking sad… What kind of a pathetic cunt am I, hey sweetheart?" He asked Minerva, hoping for an answer, "This poor honey had nothing but brutality to look forward to each day, and here I am, feeling fucking sorry for myself… fuck me… fuck me!"

Tommy shook his head in frustration and he and JoJo walked back to his mother's apartment, and then Tommy headed back to the precinct for a new day of work.

***

Tommy arrived at the empty and dark squad room about ninety minutes before his shift was to begin. Despite the long hours he had put in the day before, getting up so early, and his long walk with JoJo; a good bowl of oatmeal, and a brisk walk into the precinct, made him feel completely refreshed and ready for anything.

Tommy pulled open his case folder and went over every piece of paper, every interview, absolutely every detail he could to completely refamiliarize himself with this case. He called ADA Bradly and left him a message, letting him know he was in, and available for anything he may need, to help get this case sealed up and ready for the arraignment.

He then opened up the computer and searched out everything he could about the Woos, and the Purple Dragons gang. As he searched, he was surprised how little information was available in the NYPD's system. He then looked online and found very little there as well; a couple of articles on the war and killings, that took place between the Purple Dragons and the Ho Sing Boys, there were a couple of poorly made YouTube documentaries that glossed over the basics, but really nothing with any teeth, nothing that had any value at all for Tommy. 'Strange' he thought, 'A gang this notorious, and so little about them online or in our database.'

Detective Stein was the first to walk into the office. "Hey, Mark, good morning." Tommy said.

"Morning, Tom, how are you?"

"Doing alright my friend, I got a few hours in and I'm feeling pretty good. Hey, how did that interview go with your witness on that Macca case?" Tommy asked casually, hiding the secret interest he had in this case, and his curiosity as to what exactly would come of it.

"You're not going to believe it!" Mark began, obviously agitated over the question.

"What, what am I not going to believe?"

"Well, I bring Miss Daniels in, she's going to look at a couple of six packs (a set of six photos of possible perpetrators). She comes in, much quieter than the evening we interviewed her, and with a girlfriend in tow, you know... for support. I sit her down here at my desk and give her the first one, nope nothing, then the next, nope nothing, now these two photo arrays I am sure will hit, but nothing, I then give a third, which I thought was a stretch, and again no, nothing, you know what she says to me then?"

"No, what?"

"Our Miss Daniels says she's not sure if she can remember anything from that night, it was all such a blur, it all happened so fast. That same young lady who was so detailed, and so confident in what she saw, now developed amnesia, couldn't remember a thing."

"You buy it?"

"Not for a second, you know what I think?"

"I do know what you think, you think someone got to her."

"Bingo! And the prize goes to Detective Keane! That's exactly what I think. Everyone in the bar sees a big black guy, right, then this sweet, young woman goes out of her way to give us a very detailed description of the event and the perpetrators - - two white guys! Then, not twenty-four hours later, she can't seem to remember a thing, not a fucking thing, yeah, I think someone got ahold of her, and told her to keep her mouth shut."

"What's next?"

"I don't know. Macca is still alive, hopefully he'll wake up and shed a little light on who gave him the beating, until then, let's just hope he survives, and I'm not stuck with a fucking homicide here."

As their conversation continued, Jimmy and Doreen entered the squad room, everyone sharing their hellos, then Sergeant Browne walked in, "Good morning, all!" he said loudly in an unusually positive mood, "Hey, Tom, you speak to the Lieutenant yet?"

"Lieutenant Bricks? No, what's up?"

"Sounds like the FBI wants to fold your new homicide into an ongoing case of theirs. Captain was asking the Lu about it last night."

"They had mentioned that when they were here, but we're not doing that. It's a homicide, they stay with us, that's how it works, and they know that."

"Ah, I'm just telling you what I heard, sounds like they are adamant about it."

"Yeah, well fuck them, this is my case, and it's fuckin solved already anyway, got the perp, got a witness, complaint is drafted, it's a basically a done deal, we just need to sew it up and get it to court."

"No, no, I get all that Tom, I'm just asking if you've spoken to the Lu about it yet?"

"No, Sarge, I haven't. Thanks for the heads up though."

And as their conversation came to an end Lieutenant Bricks came walking into the squad room.

"Good morning my lovelies. Tommy, may I have a moment, please."

"Sure thing, Lu."

Lieutenant Bricks entered his office and sat down at his desk, "Close the door, please." he stated.

Tommy did and stood in front of the Lieutenants desk.

"Take a seat, Tom, I want to fill you in on some of what transpired yesterday, after you left for the morgue."

"Sergeant Browne said something about the FBI?"

"Yes, it seems the FBI, as you know has an open investigation on this Mama Woo and her brother Peter Woo, and…"

Tommy interrupted, "I know this, Lu, but I'm not getting it, you know, and they know, that a homicide like this falls to us, and again, this is basically a closed case, so what the fuck could they want?"

"I don't know Tommy, I really don't know, but they went to Captain Pileggi, and you know how he loves, I mean loves, to make mountains out of mole hills. They came to him with some nonsense about this gang being an issue of national security, and he, of course, sees politicians in his dreams, and somehow thinks getting involved in this case may actually land him some sort of notoriety. Well, in the end, that pretty little agent Kai came back with her boss, and by the time they left, they had the captain eating out of their hands."

Tommy paused for a moment, "And so, what? Case is closed, it's in the court's hands now, not a lot more to do to but button it all up, what? What does Pileggi want?"

"Well, Tom, I don't know. I guess I'm just giving you a heads up, everything you said is correct, you know it, I know it, and I'm sure the Captain knows it. I am damn sure the FBI knows it. I just wanted you to be aware, there may be some grief headed your way. These FBI fuckers are literally looking to make this a federal offense, and they may become a thorn in your side, how? I have no idea. Know I have your back 100%, but also just remember who Captain Pileggi is, remember the shit he pulled with the Sister Margaret case. Again, I'm just giving you a heads-up, Detective, just keeping you in the loop, man."

"Well thanks, Lu, I appreciate it, I do." Tommy stood and reached across the desk and shook Lieutenant Bricks' hand.

Tommy returned to the squad room and his case folders, at about 9:10 his phone began to buzz, it was ADA Bradly.

"Keane here." He answered.

"They posted bail, Detective."

"What? Over a million dollars!" Tommy asked, rather loudly, having all the heads in the room turn towards him.

"No, two hundred thousand. The judge didn't take our recommendation, he did two hundred thousand on Woo, and twenty-five thousand for Teddy Lo, and five hundred a piece for the two girls."

"So, she's out? She's out? Fuck me, well, nothing we can do about that now."

"I'm sorry, Detective Keane, we asked for a million-five, said she was a flight risk, explained how she was a leader of one of the most notorious gangs in the country, but the judge, well, he did what he did, and they posted it immediately in cash, bang - they all walked."

"Alright, well thanks for the heads up, I'm going to try and scoop up that outstanding witness slash suspect, our mysterious bearded man sometime today. I'll of course let you know how that goes, other than that is there anything you need from me at the moment, Bradly?"

"No, not just yet we'll be seeing quite a bit of one another in the next few days, and weeks, but nothing now. I would like it if you could bring the witness to my office first thing tomorrow if that works for you. I'll have the majority of my case written up and ready by then, and I'll just need her to sign her statement, and go before the grand jury, then we'll get her out of the city to a safe house until trial."

"Very good, done deal, my friend. 9:00 AM tomorrow?"

"Yes please."

"Okay, we'll be there."

***

Tommy took a deep breath and then sighed, there was nothing to be done about the lower than desired bail, and Mama Woo and Teddy being able to post it. Tommy had made the arrest, and closed the case, now it was just a matter of collecting any further evidence that may help the District Attorney's office out with their prosecution. He knew most of that would be coming from the lab and the final reports from the medical examiner's office. At this stage of the game, Tommy may not have been satisfied with the case, but hoped for something more from this bearded man, would he be an eyewitness, or would this case take a turn, and could he be the perpetrator?

Tommy looked over Li Jun's case folder, closed it, then took a look at a couple of his other cases and did a little typing in an attempt to keep them current, and up to date, with any progress he had made. At about 10:00 Stein stood and announced he was heading out for an interview and asked if anyone else needed to go out and wanted to join him, Jimmy Colletti said yes, as he had just picked up an assault on 63rd Street, from the night before and planned to meet with the victim at noon at his place of work.

Tommy and Doreen sat silently typing away on their cases. Tommy paused and got up to get himself a bottle of water, as he did, he passed Stein's desk and saw the three photo arrays sitting next to the computer monitor. Tommy picked them up and looked at each one, each array held six mug shots of known criminals from the area, all were white, Tommy immediately recognized four of the eighteen.

The first was Augustus "Gusty" Cole. Cole was a couple of years older than Tommy, and Tommy had known Gusty for about forty years. He was a very tough, very scary, man, and fit the description of one of the perpetrators young Miss Katie Daniels had given to a T. Yup, Tommy would have pulled this photo as a possible suspect as well.

In the same array was another very scary man Tommy was very familiar with, Michael Divine, a well-known criminal, and leg breaker for the mob. Michael, and his brother Jamie, who was featured on the next array, were two notorious thugs, well known all over the city for doing the violent bidding for any number of gangs and union halls all over the five boroughs. If there was anything someone who owed money or had wronged an underworld figure in some way didn't want, it was a visit from the brothers Divine.

And there, on the last array, top photo center, was an older mug shot, if Tommy guessed he would have thought it to be about sixteen years old. An approximately thirty-year-old Terry Callahan, stared up from the array. Yup, exactly what Tommy had tried not to think about two nights ago, when Katie Daniels had given her account of the assault. Tommy knew Joey Macca, he knew him for the lowlife thief and miscreant that he was, and always had been. He also knew he would be the kind of fool, the kind of stupid moron, to drop Terry Callahan's name to lend himself some street cred, or possibly get himself out of a jam. And Gusty Cole, well, Gusty was like Terry's right hand, and fit perfectly into Miss Daniels description, large, middle aged, thick necked, flat top haircut and wearing working man's attire, Yup, that described Gusty alright.

'Good job, Mark,' Tommy thought, 'I would have pulled these photos myself. But I guess it's up to Macca now. If he survives, will he point the finger at Terry and Gusty? Or maybe the Divines?' Tommy was now wholly interested in how this was going to play out, and who? Which one of these four were mixed up in this assault, if any?

As he stared at the final array with Terry's photo in it, he looked up at Doreen and asked, "Hey Doreen, you wanna take a ride and see if our bearded friend has made it to work at the liquor store yet?"

"Hmmm? Take a ride with you, grab some coffee, and pick up a filthy criminal, possible murderer, or sit here and type myself into madness? I think I will take a ride with you mister man, but you're buying the coffee!"

"Again?"

"Hey, you ask me out, you gotta pay, I ask you out, I gotta pay, that's the way it works pal."

***

10:22 AM D&B Wines and Spirits 2nd Avenue

Tommy and Doreen stood outside of the liquor store looking in for a minute to see if they could see anyone who fit the description of the man who made it out of the brothel un-apprehended two days prior. They saw two men behind the counter. One who appeared to be in his late sixties, and the other was a larger man, of the right age and size, but without a beard.

Tommy and Doreen decided they would enter the store, but rather than immediately questioning the man they would shop for a minute, then Doreen would engage the younger man in conversation.

"Good morning," The older gentleman said as Doreen and Tommy entered the store, and both Doreen and Tommy, nodded and reciprocated the greeting. Casually taking in everything the store had to offer, both Tommy and Doreen made a mental note that there was a navy pea coat hanging on a coat rack behind the counter. Once satisfied with their surroundings, they both approached the far side of the counter where the younger man stood leaning, his elbows on the counter as he wrote in some kind of logbook.

The younger man looked up from his book at Doreen, "Do you need some help?"

Doreen cocked her head slightly to one side, "I like it." She said, "I liked your beard, but I think I like you better now without it."

"Really? Well thank you, thank you very much." The man answered, a little surprised by the complement. "What can I help you with?" he then asked with a smile.

Doreen kindly smiled back and as Tommy stepped a bit closer to the counter, she softly asked, as she pulled her jacket back revealing the detective shield on her belt, "We'd really like to ask you about what happened with you over at 439 80th Street the other night, if you have a minute to spare."

The man went white as a ghost, and for a moment looked as if he was going to pass out.

"Uh, um, can, can we not do this here?" The man asked.

"Actually sir… What is you name by the way?"

"Noel, my name is Noel Fitsimmons."

Tommy interjected, "Noel, we have no intention of doing this here, you my friend are going to take a ride with us over to the 2-1, where we are going to have a long conversation."

"Please sir, ma'am, I don't want any trouble and I won't be difficult, I promise. I'll tell you everything, absolutely everything, can we please, not make a scene here, that's my father, and this is his business. I will happily leave with you now and go through whatever it is I have to go through, please just please let's not have a scene."

"I like your style, Noel. My partner and I would very much like this to go smoothly as well, so what say you grab your pea coat there and step outside with us, then we'll take you to the precinct for a nice sit down."

"Yes sir."

"And Noel."

"Yes sir?"

"Were treating you like a gentleman, don't do anything stupid to make us stop."

"No sir."

"Okay then let's go,"

"Hey Pop, I have to step out for a minute, I'll be back in a bit?"

"What? What is it now Noel? How long do you think?"

"Not long, Pop."

The three stepped outside and walked about fifty feet to where the car was parked in the bus stop, "Toss your coat on the hood Noel, and put your hands on the roof."

"Yes sir."

"Toss his coat, Doreen." Tommy asked as he patted Noel down and then cuffed him.

"It's clean." She said, and Tommy handed her the keys as he put Noel in the rear passenger side seat then walked around the car and got in the rear driver's side seat next to him, and Doreen drove them all back to the 2-1.

***

Once in the station house Tommy and Doreen took Noel straight to the box in the squad room. Tommy read him his Miranda warnings, had him sign, then got straight to the point.

"Noel, it's pretty obvious we got you, we know exactly where you were and we have as many as six witnesses putting you in that apartment at 439, so please don't jerk me around with any bullshit, just come clean with your story of the events that happened that night."

Noel cleared his throat, wiped a tear from each eye, and began. "Yes sir, yes ma'am, I went to the building, to 439, to have sex at the brothel Q, on the third floor, and... Oh god," Noel took a deep breath, "I had sex with Harmony, one of their regular girls, and I made the mistake of complaining, she, well she wasn't into it, she was, she was very tired I guess, I don't know but she, well she wasn't her usual self, she was very moody, and I complained to the boss, and demanded my money back."

"So, you were a regular, and you knew Harmony?" Tommy asked.

"Yes, yes sir, I had been there many times, once sometimes twice, a week. I was a regular there sure, and Harmony was one of my favorites. She was, oh man... she was a pretty sweet girl, but the other night she wasn't into it, and I, well as I said I complained to the boss."

"Then?" Tommy asked.

The boss gave me my money back, then went into Harmony's room and shouted at her, and then he stepped out and this well dressed fat woman, came out from another room and grabbed me by the sleeve and pulled me back into the room where she shouted at Harmony in Chinese, motioning to me as she did, then began slapping her around the room, Harmony protested, and grabbed the woman by her wrists to try and keep from being hit and the woman, oh man, well the woman shoved Harmony so hard she just flew back and went right out the open window, it all, it just all happened so quickly."

"And then" Tommy asked.

"I panicked and ran."

Li Jun

"Did you see the police downstairs?"

"Yes, sir I did, but I don't know I was already in motion man, and I wasn't stopping, I was just in such a panic, I saw Harmony on the fence downstairs and the cops across the street and well I just kept running... I'm sorry, I am so so sorry."

"Do you know the woman, the heavyset woman the pushed Harmony out the window Noel?"

"No sir, I've never seen her."

"We have all of this on tape, Noel, now I'm going to ask you to write it all down on this yellow pad, and sign it for us, don't leave anything out, write it down just the way you told us."

"Yes sir."

Noel did exactly what he was asked, Tommy and Doreen then exited the interview room and once outside Doreen raised her hand and Tommy gave her a high five, then they quietly stepped back into the squad room both knowing what had just transpired.

Noel, and the statement he had just made to the camera and on paper, was the eyewitness corroboration that ADA Bradly would need to make the case for the murder of Li Jun, by Mama Woo. There was a large amount of circumstantial evidence, and all were hoping for some solid forensics, but this eyewitness to the actual act would certainly be what made the case.

Tommy asked Doreen to run Noel for warrants and priors as he made a call to ADA Bradly, "Hey Mike it's Tommy Keane, we have an eyewitness for the Li Jun case... Yes sir, the John who made the complaint witnessed the fight and saw Mama

Woo shove Li out the window… We're running him for priors and warrants right now, what would you like me to do with him… Okay great yes, I'll get him down there tomorrow to see you, great thanks."

Tommy hung up then directed his attention to Doreen, "Okay, Doreen, so we'll book him on the misdemeanor prostitution charge, and give him a DAT, (Desk Appearance Ticket) then we'll 343 him (Non process the crime) pending his cooperation, that should satisfy our situation, and ensure his cooperation?

"Sounds good mister man, and he is eligible for a DAT, no warrants, and no priors."

"Perfect."

Tommy and Doreen booked Noel for patronizing a person for prostitution in the third degree, a class A Misdemeanor, and as Tommy filled out the paperwork he explained to Noel,

"Listen to me, Noel, and don't screw this up. If you cooperate with the district attorney's office, we will not process this crime, I'm going to give you a desk appearance ticket today, which will keep you out of central booking and off Rikers Island, but you have to do the right thing, and cooperate with the DA's office, you hear me?"

"Yes sir, I'm actually happy to help, Detective, and happy you caught up with me today, I, well that night has been haunting me, I think now, you know, by testifying, I'll be able to maybe put some of this behind me?"

"Listen, Noel, you fucked up, and got tangled up in an awful situation, but I do believe you have an opportunity to redeem yourself here, just do the right thing... here, this is ADA Bradly's number, get with him, make an appointment and do what he asks, you may be able to make all of this go away, do the right thing by that poor young girl, and keep your ass out of jail."

"Thank you, Detective Keane, I will, I will do exactly what you're telling me."

***

As Tommy walked Noel out of the precinct his phone went off. He could see it was a call from Detective Lisa Yan, "Detective Yan, how you doing?"

"I'm well, thank you, I'd like to speak to you Tommy, I know it's a little late, but have you eaten yet? Are you available for lunch today?" Lisa asked.

"Yes, I think I can meet you, everything alright? You sound a bit distressed."

"No, I'm fine, I would just like to speak with you privately, and have a longer conversation about your homicide case. I may have more light I can shed on the Woos than we were able to discuss yesterday."

"Sure, that would be great, where would you like to meet?"

"I don't know, but not down here, or in your precinct either, let's meet somewhere in between, say two o'clock? Maybe you know a place, a simple quiet diner maybe?"

"Sure, how about the Orion, it's on Second Avenue and 23rd Street."

"Okay, see you there at two."

"Looking forward to it."

Li Jun

Chapter Nine

1:54 PM Orion Diner 395 2nd Avenue.

Tommy entered the Orion and immediately saw Lisa Yan sitting at a booth in the far-right corner of the diner.

"Hey, Lisa, how you doing?"

"Good, thank you. I, I, well Tommy I want to talk to you about your case, and the Woos."

"Yeah, I got that from what you said on the phone, what exactly…"

Their conversation was interrupted by the waitress, "You two knows what yous want?" She asked with an obviously overworked and ambivalent attitude.

"Yes, I'll have a bowl of Matza Ball soup, and a diet, please."

"And I think I'll take a slice of seven-layer cake, and an unsweetened iced tea, please."

"Okay, yous got it, just be a minute."

As she walked away, Tommy started again, "So, what exactly did you want to tell me, Lisa, like I said, you sounded a little off on the phone, and you seem a little on edge now."

"Is it that obvious? Well, I'm barely cut out to be a cop, I guess it's obvious I could never go undercover, huh?... I have a lot to share, and I think I can trust you. I think, well from what I understand, you, you are a stand-up guy, Tommy, and well, I have decided to trust you with all I know, and suspect, concerning the Woos... and..." she nervously paused.

"And what?"

"Okay, let me back up a little, I have been investigating everything I can find on the Woos and the Purple Dragons for a few years now, and I don't think anyone knows more than I do. The problem is, well the problem is – they are so connected and corrupt, Tommy, I, I'm telling you, they are so deep into drugs and human trafficking, with worldwide connections, that run so deep, I mean, look at it." Lisa paused again.

"I have been tracking the Woos for over three years through our gang unit, and I have only ever seen three photos of Mama Woo, and seven of Peter Woo, and never seen either of them in the flesh. They are complete phantoms, and yet are responsible for hundreds of millions of dollars in illegal activity here in New York, San Francisco, and Canada. You, you stumbling across Mama Woo the way you did, Tommy, it's like hitting the lottery, and you think you have her but, I'm, I'm not so sure."

"What do you mean you're not so sure?"

"She made bail, right?"

"Yeah, she..."

"I know, I was there."

"You were there? At the arraignment?"

"Yeah, like I said, I've been following the Woos for the last three years, it's been a huge part of my life. I had to see what would happen, and sure enough, ADA Bradly asked for 1.5 million dollars bail, and the judge said two hundred thousand, she was out in less than an hour, and now, well, I bet we never see her again."

"You think she's gonna take flight?"

"I'm sure of it, they have the money, they have the connections, shit, if she doesn't leave the country, she'll just go underground. I haven't been able to put an eye on her for three years, no one in the gang unit has."

"Agent Kai said the same thing."

"Okay, so listen to me." Lisa Yan was already serious, but her voice lowered a bit, and took on an even more serious attitude. "Don't trust Kai, or that Conroy, or any other FBI agent that may come to you about this case."

"In general, I tend not to trust anyone, Lisa, but what exactly are you getting at, you know something?"

Lisa paused and took a breath as the waitress approached and served them their soup and cake.

"I don't know, that's my problem, but I do suspect. I have intercepted messages and overheard conversations on wires talking about the Woos having agents in their pockets, and I hate to say it, but NYPD too. I have no names, I only have inferences, but one thing I can tell you, is every time we seem to get ahold of something solid on the Woos, or the Purple Dragons, Michelle Kai shows up, and pulls our investigation into one of the FBIs, and 1PP (NYPD Headquarters) always seems to give in to their requests – always."

"Do you think there is a corrupt cop working in 1PP giving you up to the FBI?"

"Oh, I have no idea, really no clue at all, but I can tell you, if you sniff around anything concerning the Woos, Agent Michelle Kai, will show up… Just like she did for you yesterday, Tommy, let me ask you, did you notify the FBI? I know I didn't, yet she showed up, didn't she?"

"Yes, she did, didn't she?"

***

Tommy and Lisa ate their lunch and as they finished their conversation, Lisa said she would deliver anything and everything she had on the Woos. Many of her notes she had begun to keep in a private file, for fear of corrupt police personnel, or FBI agents, who might get their hands on them. This offering up of secret files made Tommy truly take notice and believe he could trust his new acquaintance, Detective Lisa Yan.

But where this case, the case that as far as he was concerned was already closed the day prior, where this was going is what was intriguing Tommy now. What had he become a part of? Murderous international smugglers, crooked cops, and FBI agents.

'What is this now?' he thought.

Chapter Ten

Tommy found himself unsure of what to make of this case. It appeared he had the proverbial 'can of worms' in his hands; A beautiful child, sold into a life of sex slavery, brutalized, tortured, and now dead. One of the most sought-after Chinese gangsters in the city, possibly the world, free on bail. A witness willing to attest to the horrors she, and the dead girl lived, yet unwilling to speak to fellow Chinese officers, or FBI agents. A seemingly sharp detective holding secret files.

This was an unusual case for Tommy. He was well versed in crime, had investigated just about every sort of atrocity imaginable over the years, but here he was in a world he didn't understand. A community, a culture, that was somehow completely separate from anything he had ever experienced in his life. Here he was almost forty-seven years old, had been to Chinatown dozens of times, but outside of eating Chinese food, he really knew nothing of Chinese people, much less the workings of their community's underworld.

As was customary, he reached out to one of his oldest friends from the neighborhood. In this situation, it was one he hadn't seen in ten to fifteen years. His dear friend from childhood, Eddie, the youngest of the two Yee brothers, who grew up on the same block as Tommy.

Eddie, and his older brother, Johnny, grew up on 88th Street with Tommy. Their family owned and operated a laundry just off of Second Avenue for over thirty years. Together they attended grade school, played ball in the streets, and went to Wagner Junior High School together. Although they always remained friends, both Eddie and Johnny stopped hanging around the neighborhood when they entered high school. Johnny attended Stuyvesant, a well-respected public preparatory school, and the younger Eddie studied at The Bronx High School of Science; coincidently the same High School Detective Lisa Yan would attend seven years after Eddie's graduation.

Tommy pulled his phone from his pocket, 'Please let this still be your number Ed.' "Beep Beep Beep -- The number you have dialed is no longer in service."

This was an inconvenience, but he knew where Eddie worked, he currently owned and operated a chain of three rotisserie chicken restaurants in the city, so Tommy simply looked one up on his phone and hit the call button.

"Yes hello, may I speak to Eddie Yee please? – Okay, do you think you could have him call me when he gets back, please? – Yes, tell him to call Tommy Keane at 212-555-2368 -- Yes, thank you."

Not two minutes went by when Tommy's phone went off.

***

Tommy arrived at The Globe Pub, 158 East 23rd Street, and found Eddie waiting for him at the bar with a cold pint of beer in front of him. The Irish bartender was saying something to Eddie that made him throw his head back and laugh, and Tommy decided he hadn't changed much since the last time he had seen him.

Eddie was still in good shape and was dressed casually in a simple navy crew neck sweater, blue jeans, and white Adidas. As Tommy approached, Eddie stood up and with a broad smile and a heavy old-school New York accent spoke,

"Tommy, good to see ya, pal. Man, it's been forever… how you doing? Cookie? The kids? Or is it just the kid?"

They shook hands and then embraced.

"Doing good, Eddie, and you're lookin' well, don't think you've aged a day since the last time I saw you. And yeah, just one kid, our Caitlin, and she's a great girl. Cookie and I have been divorced for about ten years now, but we see each other all the time, and she's doing well."

Eddie sat back down on the bar stool and Tommy pulled the one next to him out and hung his coat on the back. Tommy signaled to the bartender and ordered a Budweiser and a second beer for Eddie.

"Oh sorry, I feel I should know that?"

"Nah, don't be sorry, nothing to be sorry about, it's been years."

The two continued catching up for about ten minutes when Eddie got to the heart of their meeting, "So Tommy, what can I do for you? You said you wanted to talk about some case of yours? So what? How can I help?"

"Well, it turns out, you and Johnny are the only Chinese friends I got," he sheepishly grinned, "So I wanted to reach out, tell you about what's going on with this case, and at the risk of coming off like some kinda racist prick, tap into you a bit, see if you have any kind of info you can help me out with ... because I really don't know anything about Chinese culture in this city – And to be very honest, although there are some Chinese detectives helping me out, this case has got some bite to it. I know it runs deep, and I don't know anything about these detectives that are assigned or if I can trust them ... So, so here we are Ed – Come let's grab a seat away from the bar and let me tell you what's going on."

They grabbed their beers and walked back to the rear of the bar and took a seat at a table under a stained-glass window.

"Well, you know you can ask me anything, and whatever you say goes no further." Eddie stated as they sat.

"That goes without saying, and that's why we're here, if I didn't think I could trust you I would have never asked to meet."

"So, what you got going? Something involving some Chinese obviously?"

"Yeah, well it started out with a dead prostitute. We think she was thrown from a window... awful story, poor young girl never had a chance. Sounds like her parents sold her to some snake heads in China, but regardless. We think she was nineteen, pretty, skinny little girl, getting pimped out by this brother and sister team, who it turns out are so deep into this human trafficking and importing of fentanyl, the NYPD's Asian Gang unit, the DEA, Immigration, and the FBI, have all been tracking them for the last couple of years. Sadly, no one has been able to catch them with anything, they're pros, keep away from all the product, they're like..."

"You're onto the Woos, aren't you?"

"So, you know them?"

"Well, I certainly don't know them personally, but I know who you're talking about – they are the worst of the worst, Tommy."

"So, you're familiar with them, and the Purple Dragons then too?"

"Yeah, well they are one in the same basically."

"Please, anything you can tell me -- I have information, but I don't know any of these other detectives, or any of the feds, that are supposed to be enhancing this case. And I really don't know who I can trust and who I can't, so anything, no matter how small, let me hear it, anything could help."

"Alright well, really, I gotta tell you I don't know much. You know my folks came straight to New York after escaping from China at the end of the sixties, and they, especially my pop is one of the most patriotic, pro-America guys you could meet. And I -- Johnny and I, were raised with a disdain, and outright hatred, for our old country... nothing but awful stories of just how unbelievably oppressed our people were over there. Shit, outside of Bruce Lee, there was nothing we wanted to know about anything that came out of China, and growing up in Yorkville, and going to Wagner, almost none of our friends were

Chinese, until I got to high school. Bronx Science had a lot of Chinese students, but as you know, if you remember, before high school, we just had our street friends, and our school friends, and we spent every day after school working in the laundry, helping out our folks, all that aside, I can share a bit, maybe more than you know, but probably not more than the FBI or the DEA."

"Anything, Eddie, even if you think it's nothing, anything."

"Well, the Woos – These Woos, it's a very common name, but these Woos, are an awful pair, like I said, the worst of the worst. You know Chinese organized crime, the Tongs are huge, much larger than any of that Italian shit we love to watch on TV, and they go way back, I mean a thousand, no, thousands of years, they have their fingers into everything in China. Remember, China is an authoritarian communist country, so the Tongs have to be able to do business within a country run by a government that murders and enslaves its own people."

Eddie paused and took a swig of his beer then continued.

"I mean America, Canada, Europe... C'mon man, these countries are like a candy land to the Tongs, and the Tongs, well you see they may be, no, let me make this point, they *are* the smartest of the organized crime groups in the world. You see, they make money from everything, they have their fingers in absolutely everything, and they keep the lowest of low profiles. I mean there isn't a part of Chinese culture that's not touched or taxed by one of the Tongs. That's why, Tommy, that's why you don't see any Chinese immigrants working in my restaurants, I only hire Mexicans and Guatemalans. I can't, I won't get mixed up with any of them, you pay a guy ten, fifteen, dollars an hour and he's got to pony-up 80-90% of that back to the people that brought him here, it's slavery, fucking slavery."

Eddie took another sip from his beer.

"And these Purple Dragons, and the Woos, well these people you're looking at are actually shunned by the Tongs. They're considered too wild and uncivilized, rumor is, and again, it's just something I heard ... but rumor is, the Woos had a mini war with one of the main Chinatown Tongs, and supposedly to end this war, and to keep business moving, Peter Woo and Mama Woo paid up a hundred million to be considered legitimate entities within their Tong world."

"A hundred million?" Tommy asked in disbelief.

"I bet they make three times that a year, Tommy, fuck me ... maybe five times that?"

"Really?"

"Easily, forget about all the drugs, which they bring into America by the ton, but the people? Human trafficking is the crime that pays and pays and pays, many of these people sell themselves into slavery to get here, promised a better life, then like I said, are sold to restaurants, factories, brothels, whatever. To work themselves to death to try and pay their debts to these snake heads, tongs, gangs? It never ends, internationally it's a multibillion-dollar business."

"And these Woo's are taking this business for all it's worth, I know, three to five hundred million a year sounds insane, but ask your FBI agents, I bet I'm not far off. Again, let me repeat myself, they are the worst of the worst. Be careful - they have influence, they have connections and fuck do they have money… Be careful, Tommy, these are truly dangerous people you are dealing with."

"Yeah well, I promised this young girl. I promised her I'd get to the bottom of this and get some retribution for this short and awful life she was forced into, and I, I intend to make good on it."

"Ahh, this young prostitute got lucky, she hooked into that Keane sense of honor I see -- Just be fucking careful pal, I'm telling you, these Woos are wild, unpredictable, and dangerous as fuck!"

Chapter Eleven

Tommy's day was over, and he thought about heading over to Bailey's Corner Pub on the way home but wasn't up for seeing Molly. He thought a good night's sleep would do him better than a couple beers and some whiskey would, so he headed straight home. Besides, he had packed a lot into his head about this Li Jun case, and the Woos, and now crooked cops and FBI agents, yeah 'Some sleep' he thought 'Let's sleep on this kid and see how we feel about it in the morning.'

Tommy walked into his mother's apartment and found his mother sitting in her recliner watching TV with his little dog JoJo, on her lap, a cigarette in one hand and a glass of scotch in the other. JoJo immediately jumped up and ran to Tommy as he locked the door.

"How you doin, Ma?"

"Good, Tommy, good, how are you tonight, Tommy, did you have a fine day today, Tommy?"

"Yes, ma'am, I did, I saw and caught up with Eddie Yee today, Ma."

Maria Keane turned in her chair to look up at Tommy, "Eddie Yee? Tommy, I haven't seen any of the Yee's in years and years, how was he, Tommy? And his family?"

"He's doing great, Ma, and so is his family, they own a home, actually a couple of homes in Flushing and out on the Island and are doing just fine, Ma."

"That's nice to hear, Tommy, nice, nice family the Yee's."

Tommy got himself some water and sat on the couch and chatted a bit with his mother until about 10:12 pm when his phone went off to a number he didn't recognize, "Keane here," he answered.

A frantic, almost indiscernible, voice on the other end spoke. "Help me, Keane, I need help, I afraid Keane, help!"

Tommy immediately realized what was happening, it was Min. She was crying, and obviously terrified, and called the only number she had, "Please, Keane, I afraid they kill me!"

Tommy was able to calm her down a bit and find out that she was in the hotel that she had been left in the day before, and she was calling from a room two stories above the floor she was staying on. This he immediately found out belonged to two tourists from Wyoming, after Min had handed the phone to a rather excited young man, who gave Tommy his room number and what few details he had. Tommy informed the tourist of who he was, and not to allow Min to leave his room, to comfort her as much as he could, and that he would be there as quickly as possible.

Maria Keane stared up at Tommy who was now standing as he had this conversation and asked, "Is everything okay, Tommy?"

"Yes, Ma. All is okay. I just need to go check on a witness. I'm sorry dear, I don't know when I'll be back Ma, but don't worry I shouldn't be long."

He kissed his mother on top of her head and headed right back out the door, as he did, he called ADA Bradly on his cell, "Pick up Bradly, pick up." He mumbled out loud as he stepped out onto the street and ran down to First Avenue, Bradly didn't pick up and his phone went to voice mail,

"Mike, this is Tommy Keane, call me back immediately. I need to confirm something with you!" He raised his hand to hail a cab as he reached the avenue.

A yellow cab pulled up and Tommy hoped in, as he did the cab driver asked, "Where you goin'?"

"You a good driver?" Tommy asked.

"Yes, of course I'm a good driver!" The cabbie answered rather miffed by the question.

"Glad to hear it pal, Detective, NYPD," Tommy tapped his detective shield against the bullet proof partition for the cabbie to see, "I need you to take me to a hotel in Midtown, I'm not sure which one, but this is an emergency, so you're gonna stop at every light, but then go right on through while I try and find out exactly where we are going – You got that? Any questions?"

The cabbie paused for a moment not sure exactly to do or say, but then came back with "You got the right guy!" and hit the gas.

Tommy called Mark Stein, next but just as he could hear Mark's phone ring, he had a return call come back from ADA Michael Bradly, "Mike! Thanks for getting back!"

"What's up, Detective, you sound stressed?"

"Listen our witness, Min, is in some sort of trouble. I'm in a cab heading downtown, where exactly is she lodged?"

"The Howard Johnson's on 8th, and 52nd, room 203."

"Cool, I'll let you know what's up as soon as I do."

"Okay, thanks!"

"I gotta go, I got someone calling me." Tommy hung up and answered a return call from Mark Stein.

"You called, Tom?"

"Yeah, Mark, I got the info I needed from the ADA. I'm headed down to the hotel on 8th where my witness is being lodged… she called saying she was in trouble and in some other room other than hers, not sure what's going on, but I needed to know the hotel, and wasn't sure if you knew it or not, thanks for getting back right away."

"Hey, no problem, man, do you need some help? You okay, you know where you're going, right? Howard Johnson's on 8th?"

"I think it'll be fine, I just gotta get there and find out what's happening, or what spooked her, she's in a room on the fourth floor with some fucking tourists, I'll hit you up when I arrive and assess the situation."

"Okay then, don't be shy, you need something I'm here for you."

"Thanks, Mark, I appreciate it." Then turning his attention to the cabbie, "Howard Johnson's on 8th and 52nd Street!"

"I know it!" The cabbie replied with a large smile and an excited look on his face.

The cabbie was right, Tommy did hail the 'right guy' for the job, he drove like a bank robber, weaving in and out of traffic, the blocks counting down seemingly ten at a time, 79th Street, then 68th, then 53rd and they pulled up to the hotel in a matter of minutes.

"Thanks, Pal, and good job. You need anything from me or the police, you give me a call." Tommy said as he handed the cabbie a $20 bill and his card, then before the cabbie could get "Thanks" out of his mouth Tommy was rushing into the hotel lobby.

As he entered, he held his shield in his hand passing the young woman at the desk, "Detective, NYPD, I'm going to the fourth floor, you will hear from me shortly."

The young woman shouted "sir, sir." After him but he made it into the elevator before she could stop him.

Tommy got off the elevator and made his way to room 404, and gently knocked.

"Yes?" Was the response.

"Detective Keane, NYPD." Tommy said rather softly so not to have his voice heard by any of the other rooms on the floor. The door slowly opened, and Tommy showed his detectives shield to a young man of about thirty.

"Well, hello, hello Detective, my name is John Rutter, and this here is my wife, Ashley, and here is the girl that called you, Min. I know you know her, I'm not sure exactly what is going on here, sir, but she says her room was broken into by some bad men, and she's pretty shook up about it."

"Thank you so much for your help, Mr. Rutter," Tommy nodded at his wife, "Mrs. Rutter," as he passed, her then made his way over to Min who was sitting on the second of the two queen beds that were in the room. As he approached her, she leapt up and threw her arms around him tightly.

"I so happy you come, I, I, I all alone here, and they come for me, they come to kill me, I so scared, I so, so scared!" Min buried her head in Tommy's chest as she spoke in a panicked tone.

"Relax, Min, I'm here now, and you're safe. Tell me now, tell me what happened, who came, who did you see? What did they do?"

Min held Tommy tight for a few more seconds then slowly released him, "I don't know who, I no see no one, but – I go for some food, I take money you give and go for some food outside, when I come back to room, door broken, lock broken, I, I see this and I run, but no elevator, so I take stairs but afraid to go outside, so go up to this floor, and see these people in hall so I ask and beg them let me in. I say I afraid and they say okay and let me in, then I call you, and then, then you come, thank you, thank you, you save Min."

As Min continued John interjected, "Yes sir, that's about exactly how it happened on our end, sir, she came out of the staircase door and we had just come off the elevator, and well, here you are now." John and Ashley were deeply concerned for

Min, but at the same time had these strange looks on their faces as if this was somehow the highlight of their trip to New York City. Being involved with an actual victim, in a state of emergency, having to call a police detective to her aid from their room, was a story they knew they would be telling for years to come back home in Cody, Wyoming.

As John went on talking, Tommy was distracted by his phone. He could see it was Mark calling him again, "Hey, Mark, what's up?" Tommy asked.

"Hey, I just arrived, I'm downstairs, where are you?"

"Wow, that was quick…you couldn't wait for me to call you?"

"I could, but I wouldn't. I didn't want you getting mixed up in something on your own. Where are you?"

"Room 404."

Tommy sat Min back down on the bed, "Relax, Min, you are safe now," then turning his attentions to John and Ashley, "Can I ask the two of you to look after her for a minute? Another detective has arrived, and we're going to go and look at her room. See if we can figure out exactly what's going on here." There was knock at the door, "That'll be him now."

***

Tommy and Mark exited the stairway door, both with their weapons drawn, and made their way to room 203. As they approached, they could see the door was open, and then observed that it had been kicked in and the metal door lock and jamb were bent and broken. The detectives took cover on either side of the door… hearing nothing, Tommy poked his head in and announced, "NYPD, nobody move, we're coming in, announce yourself, let us know you're here!" There was no response and Tommy entered the room first.

The room was empty, nothing in the room but a couple pieces of Min's clothing, and some old fast-food packaging, but everything had none the less been turned upside down.

Tommy and Mark relaxed.

"They knew where she was, Mark," Tommy said looking at him in disbelief, "How could they know?"

"Only one way, Tom… Someone told them. And it wasn't me, I knew where she was, and your ADA knew where she was, but even you didn't know."

"Bradly? Wow, I can't see it, but what the fuck is going on here, man?"

"Somebody doesn't want this girl making it to court, and that someone has got some connections."

"Yes sir, this shit runs deep. Okay, I'm gonna get her out of here, I'm gonna stick her somewhere safe, where no one but me knows where she's at – You do me a favor, Mark?"

"Anything."

"Can you get with hotel security see what they have on video? I'm going to get our Min together, then we'll meet downstairs and I'll stash her away in another hotel. We'll see if we can put anything together on exactly what happened here."

"You got it, I'll meet you downstairs as soon as you make it down."

Tommy headed back up to the room, with what few belongings she had left in room 203, to where Min waited with the tourists. Mark headed down to the front desk, identified himself and described what had happened. He was led to the security office, where a very nice, young woman helped cue up the surveillance video, from the last couple hours.

Tommy and Min soon joined them in the security office and together viewed the footage. Within a few moments they saw four Chinese men arrive, two of which were very well-built body builders. They walked right past the desk as the other two men remained in the lobby.

"They – them, them Chus!" Min stated in a panicked voice.

"You recognize them?" Tommy asked as he watched the video, then repeated the question, looking at Min this time, "You know these men, Min?"

"Yes! Them Chus!"

"Purple Dragons?"

"Yes, Chus… Purple Dragons. One Marty, and one Tony Chu, I know them, they Mama and Peter Woo's men, all Purple Dragon, Woo's men." She stuttered, her small body shaking.

"I'm going to take you someplace new, Min, someplace nobody knows but me, do you understand? I promised I would keep you safe, and I failed here, Min, I failed because I trusted someone I shouldn't have, but no more Min, I promise I will keep you safe, I promise, okay?"

"Please." Was Min's one word reply.

Everyone paused for a moment while they continued to watch the Chu brothers on the CCTV, then Mark spoke up, "What next, Tom?"

"I'm going to get this young lady a new room somewhere where only I know where she is. Other than that, there isn't much else to do. New shift starts in a few hours, and I have to bring Min to see ADA Bradly, at 9:00 AM, where he will have some explaining to do as to how anyone would know where Min was located... This is very unnerving, Mark, no one should have known where to find her, how did these guys track her down so quickly?

"Has to be an inside connection." Mark replied.

Chapter Twelve

Tommy got another room not far from where they currently were. He instructed Min not to leave, under any circumstances, and said he would return for her in a few hours. He warned her again not to open the door for anyone but him. Tommy headed back to his mother's apartment where he showered and shaved, then dressed. He then packed a small bag with fresh underwear and a clean shirt.

His mother, Maria, was up due to Tommy's busyness, so he asked if he could take one of her velour, warm-up suits and some socks to his witness. Min was a bit smaller than Maria, but not so small that she would be swimming in her clothing.

He made his way back to the hotel where he had stashed Min, then sat with her until the morning to ensure she felt safe. He wanted to keep her calm until he needed to escort her to ADA Bradly's office in the morning.

***

Tommy called Lieutenant Bricks just before 8 AM and explained the situation and the details from the night before. Lieutenant Bricks told Tommy to do whatever he needed to, and that he would be signed in. Afterwards, Tommy and Min headed down to the Court house on Center Street and to the office of ADA Bradly.

As soon as they arrived, Tommy, in a very stern manner, told the story of the previous night and wanted to know how anyone could have found where Min had been lodged. This was, after all, supposed to be the New York City District Attorney's Office protecting a witness.

Bradly was stunned to hear the news and asked why he wasn't immediately notified the night before, Tommy's simple response was, "I couldn't take that chance."

ADA Bradly was insulted to know Tommy may now doubt his integrity, but also understood they had almost lost a witness, just a few short hours before, to a criminal gang who would have most certainly murdered this girl. He realized that there was a breach of security, most likely right here in his own office, that put Min's life at risk, as well as the case.

"I, I'm sorry, Detective. I will see what I can do to find out what happened here yesterday."

With that, the City of New York swore out its complaint against Mama and Peter Woo, as well as a complaint against Teddy Lo and the Chu Brothers, who Tommy asked ADA Bradly to write out arrest warrants for, so he might be able to track them down and not have to ask for warrants in the future.

All of this took a couple of hours and when it was all done Tommy took Min across the street to Thailand Restaurant. The restaurant sat on the corner of Bayard and Baxter, where they sat and ate chicken in yellow curry, with coconut rice. It was the first time in Min's life she sat in a real restaurant and eaten that way.

Once they were finished at the restaurant, Tommy brought Min back to ADA Bradly's office, and she testified before the grand jury against Mama Woo, Teddy Lo, and the Chu brothers, and an hour later, Noel arrived and told his story to the grand jury. Their combined testimony resulted in indictments for both Mama Woo and Teddy Lo, later that afternoon.

After leaving the courthouse, Tommy took Min shopping, he bought her a bunch of snacks and drinks, and some simple clothing and toiletries then took her back to the hotel, where he again instructed her to wait for him to visit again, as he was leaving, Min, simply said "Thank you Keane." But those three words hit Tommy hard, as he looked into her dark eyes, he could tell just how heartfelt and honest, they were.

***

Tommy made it back to the 2-1 at about 4:35 PM, he headed up to the Squad Room, and informed both Sergeant Browne and Lieutenant Bricks what had transpired over the last couple of days.

After that, he sat at Colletti's desk, opposite Doreen Doyle, who was typing away finishing up one of her cases and ran through the whole story again with her.

"Wow sounds like you grabbed a tiger by the tail with this case, mister man. So, what you think? Could it be the FBI, or maybe some cop down at the ADA's office, dropping a dime on your witness?"

"I have no idea, Doreen, but this shit has really got a hook in me now. I mean this is, was, a closed case, right? but there seems to be a whole lot more to these Woos than just pimping and a dead prostitute. I wish I knew; I truly do."

"Yeah, I'd like to know why the FBI is so uptight about this case, again, you closed it, the night of, by arrest. It doesn't get any easier or more open and shut than that."

"Nah, there's something to this, Doreen, I don't know what it is, but I don't like it, I don't like it one bit."

And with that Tommy hopped up from his seat.

"Where you off to, mister man?"

"I need to check on something, I'll be back in a bit."

"See ya later alligator." Doreen said as Tommy walked out of the squad room door with a very pensive look on his face. As he hit the stairs, he put a call into his old friend Roya Sarhadi.

"Hey, Tommy, how you doing?"

"Hey, Roya, how you doing today kid?"

"Not bad, what can I do for you, Tommy?"

"I'd like to take you to dinner tonight if you're available dear. I have, well I'm sorry, it's not a social call. I have another problem - situation, I'd like to know if you can help me out with?"

"I am available. I'll be out of here at five, and can be pretty much anywhere by six, does that work for you?"

'How about we do 6:30 and let's say Pinocchio's, on First Avenue, that work?

"That's the little place off of 91st, right?"

"That's the place."

"Cool, I've never been in there, this will be a treat! See you at 6:30 then."

"See you there, and thanks, Roya."

"Of course."

Tommy hung up and made his way down to the precinct's property room, where everything taken into custody regarding evidence and prisoners' personal belongings are held.

He asked the property officer for the two cell phones and the tablet he had vouchered two days before, as well as a larger paper envelope to put them all in. Tommy signed everything out, thanked the officer, and headed back up to the squad room. He re-joined Doreen and banged away at a couple more of his other cases, while continuing to chat with her about the Woo case.

During this time, Tommy asked Doreen if she could help work some of her computer magic and try and find anything and everything on Marty and Tony Chu.

"But of course, Tommy, I'd do anything for you, but especially for this case, love to see what's gonna come of it in the end."

***

Li Jun

6:22 PM Pinocchio Restaurant 1748 1ˢᵗ Avenue.

As Tommy approached Pinocchio's, he saw Roya exiting a cab that had just stopped on the corner. She shut the cab door, turned, and immediately saw Tommy. She grinned and when they both met, gave him a quick hug.

"So, you've never been here before?" Tommy asked, as he nodded toward the restaurant door.

"No, never."

"It's good stuff, I promise, they do it right here."

As they entered, a tall man, with black, wavy hair and Buddy Holly glasses, was looking down at his podium. Without looking up, he asked, "Do you have reservations?"

"You need reservations for this dump?" Tommy answered.

The man looked up and smiled. "Tommy, oh man it's been so long, how are you?" The two men shook hands and then embraced.

"Doing good, Mark, hope you are as well?"

"Yes, sir, yes sir we are doing very well, thank you. Uh! So good to see you!"

"Mark, this is my friend, Roya."

"Hello, Roya! Any friend of Tommy's is a friend of mine, please, please come in, will it be just the two of you today?"

"Yes, sir, just the two of us."

"Very good, very good, how about here by the window, will this work?"

'Of course, wherever you like, Mark, we're easy."

Once they were seated, and the small talk with Mark was over, Roya began.

"So, this isn't a social call you say, what have you gotten mixed up in now that you need some help?" she smiled up at Tommy.

"Read the menu, see what you'd like, and I'll explain."

Tommy gave her a detailed run down of what had happened with the Li Jun case, and everything he had put together regarding the Woos and the Purple Dragons.

"The Purple Dragons? You know that's from Ninja Turtles, right?"

"Yes, and I remember you and Caitlin watching them when you were kids." Tommy smiled with a touch of sadness, "Trust me, this gang is much worse than the ones from Ninja Turtles. Now as I mentioned, this case is growing legs of its own, and there is a lot more involved than a madame murdering one of her prostitutes." He took a sip of water and continued, "I think there may be some Police, or FBI, involved… It turns out this is a multi-billion-dollar business, and these Woos are making hundreds of millions a year, for their part in it. And sadly, I have no back, really, no one I can trust to run with on this investigation, so here I am again, asking if you can possibly help me out. Maybe pry open this door of secrecy for me just enough to let some light in… I know that the Hayden Jon Marshall case took a toll on you, so please don't be shy to tell me no, I would completely understand."

Roya paused for a moment, "That last case I helped you with was brutal, absolutely brutal. I cried for weeks after that, but you know what? That was also the most important thing I have ever done in my life, and I would do it a hundred times over for you, Tommy. So here, right now - right away, I will say yes. I will do whatever I can to help you out. What do you have that can get me started? Do you have some emails? Websites? What?"

Tommy leaned in a little, "I have two cell phones and a tablet."

"Really?... Cool!"

"I thought you may like that; they will work, right? I mean, you'll be able to get into them?"

"Absolutely, may take a bit, but if you physically have them - it should be no problem for me to get into them and retrieve the data, then I will be able to do some serious digging for you."

"Okay, well that's awesome news. The only thing is I have to get these back to the property clerk as soon as possible."

"Not a problem. I'll give them back to you in a few hours, maybe the next day from when you give them to me. I hopefully will be able to tap into them and clone them into a separate device, then not only retrieve data whenever we like but be able to monitor any incoming or outgoing data from these, and any other linked devices. Possibly be able to reach into other devices that are in contact or trying to contact these devices."

"I'm completely lost, but it sounds like you think you can break into these fairly easily, and then be able to reach into other devices from other gang members?"

"Yes, exactly."

"It's really that easy?"

"The cloning will be easy, the hacking into other devices may not be, but once I get in, I think I should be able to get into a lot of information that you will like. I'm curious now, and you don't have to tell me, but who will you give this information to? How will you be able to use it, I mean just like last time, this will all be illegally obtained information."

"Well, I have a thought on that. I actually have two people in mind, we'll again drop some anonymous tips, to these trustworthy individuals, and hopefully this investigation will nab some truly vicious savages."

Mark interrupted them to take their order. Together they shared some bruschetta to start, Roya ordered the penne ala vodka and Tommy the chicken parmigiana, before they continued with their conversation.

"So, when can you get me these devices?"

"I have them here with me now."

"Oh wow, okay cool, so we are ready to rock then. Awesome! I'll take them home tonight, and hopefully if I have everything I need at home, I'll return them to you tomorrow morning? Will that work?"

"That, Roya, sounds like perfection." Tommy said with a broad smile.

Tommy liked this, he knew he shouldn't be getting Roya involved in these cases, but he had the utmost confidence in her abilities. He also knew he was onto something, as Doreen had said earlier, he "Had a tiger by the tail" and he was determined to do as much damage to this beast as he possibly could, hoping not to be bitten in the process.

Roya and Tommy ate their meals and the conversation swayed to other parts of their lives, as they talked about their past, and their families. Once they were finished, they walked home to 88th Street and to the building they both grew up in, Roya now in possession of Mama Woo's cell phone as well as Teddy Lo's cell phone and tablet.

Chapter Thirteen

Roya wasted no time once she got home to her, and her mother's, apartment. Although the horrors of what she had discovered, while hacking into Derek Spree's disgusting world, during the Hayden Jon Marshall case nearly shattered her emotionally; she thought it was the most important thing she had ever done in her life. Over the last couple of months, she had thought about that case and her contribution to the destruction of Spree's child trafficking ring. She had dabbled with social activism, thought she had taken a stand against injustices in the past, but her contribution to the Hayden Jon Marshall case was something real. Being able to see and read about the aftereffect, the arrests made, and the children saved, had given Roya a new and profound respect for police officers and the work they do every day.

Roya was more than eager to help Tommy out again; in fact, she was downright excited to dig into this new assignment she had received.

Roya closed and locked the door to her bedroom, then retrieved an old blue 1970's hard shelled suitcase from under her bed. Here she stored all sorts of old and new bits of computer hardware. She smiled when she realized she did indeed have a few old cell phones she had saved in the mix, as well as two old laptops.

Within minutes she had the sim cards out of the phones Tommy had given her and had them cloned onto the older phones she had found in the suitcase; she also downloaded every bit of information off of Teddy Lo's tablet onto one of the laptops.

Before she knew it, it was 1:00 AM. She didn't know how the time flew by so quickly, but she had set up three secure systems to be able to read all incoming and outgoing messages from each of the devices, without being detected. She had also retrieved and began translating messages via two different top rated translation programs. Right in front of her were thousands of text messages and emails between these devices, and links to numerous other addresses. She began compiling a list of names and numbers, as well as IP addresses, used by everyone attached to said addresses.

The information was overwhelming; however, the quantity was not surprising at all to Roya. Hacking, after all, was her profession, and she knew there would be miles of information available once she cloned these devices and began digging into them. A hurdle she didn't expect though was the translation, it seemed her translation programs were only picking up bits and pieces of these messages. Some, if they were short and simple, were easy to understand. However, most made no sense at all, and were simply not able to be translated.

Roya knew immediately her problem was going to be either that these messages were being sent in code, or in a dialect unrecognized by the programs, or a combination of both. After all, these were criminals, and absolutely everything in their lives was a dangerous secret, secrets they would regularly kill to keep.

At this late hour, Roya decided she had done enough, and that she would return the devices Tommy had given her first thing in the morning.

Although she had no information to give Tommy at that moment, she knew she had secured a virtual gold mine of evidence, that she would be able to share in the next few days. And once her hacks on some of these unknown IP addresses came through, the possibilities were endless. Yes, Roya went to bed very satisfied with herself that night.

***

Roya's eye's snapped open. She had set her alarm for 6:00 AM, to be sure to catch Tommy before he left for work, to return the cell phones and tablet she had cloned just hours before.

She reached for her phone and sent a text to Tommy, "Morning, are you up?" before she sat up in bed and stretched her back out as she sat on its edge.

Her phone buzzed, "Yes, I am, heading out with JoJo, what's up?"

"Give me a minute, and I'll join you."

"Very good."

Roya threw on a simple outfit of jeans, a t-shirt, a hoodie, and some converse. She stuffed the phones and tablet back into the envelope they came in and grabbed her jacket and headed down the stairs. As she made it to the first floor, she could see

Tommy from behind through the windows of the doors, as he stood outside with little JoJo.

As she pushed open the second door, leading to the building's stoop, she shouted "Gold mine!" to Tommy.

Tommy turned and smiled, "Gold mine? I like the sound of that! So, it worked out well then, whatever it is you did?"

"Yes!" They both began slowly walking JoJo up the block, "I knew the cloning would be simple, and I've already downloaded thousands of messages between these devices, and numerous other devices. My next hurdle will be to track and discern who these other devices belong to and where they are coming from, as far as IP addresses, then I hope to be able to hack into several of them. I mean, I have already retrieved a ton of messages and emails that I have to guess will be invaluable to you, but once I begin hacking into these other devices, well the amount of information we will be able to gain will be simply endless."

"Invaluable and endless!... I'm liking the sound of this, sweet girl!"

"We may have a problem though."

"No problems, I was loving where this was going, why you tellin' me we have problems?"

"Well, we have a massive amount of information - the problem is it's all in Chinese of course, so we can't simply read it. I've tried translating much of it already, through two different programs I have, both of which are the most reliable and highest rated available, but it turns out either they are going back and forth in some kind of code, or in an undetectable dialect, or quite possibly both. So, it's going to be difficult to retrieve a lot of what we already have, I'm not saying impossible yet, but certainly difficult."

Roya took a breath.

"I can hack into anything, Tommy, given the right amount of time. I can get into anything. The problem here will be understanding the language, and then breaking their code, if they are using one, here I will be at a loss."

"You just keep gathering the info, Roya, I'll find a way to break any codes and crack any dialects we need to get into. And good job kid, I knew if anyone could help me with this, you'd be able to."

Roya's heart filled with joy and pride as those words left Tommy's mouth. She was monetarily rewarded greatly by the company she worked for, but this work, this work was something different. It wasn't the excitement of doing something illegal, it was the simple fact that she was helping to do real good in the world that thrilled her, as well as being thanked and acknowledged by a man she had looked up to her entire life.

"Okay, Tommy, I'm your girl. I have to go to work today, but once I'm in, I'm going to take a half day. I'll see what I can do to gather as much data as I can. I'll keep collecting it and download it all onto thumb drives for you, and once I get my bearings on exactly what's going on here, we'll be able to start monitoring these people in real time. Also, I'll see what I can do to discern any patterns in their messaging and find a better way to translate. Hopefully, I can get into any of the codes they may be using. What is your schedule like today?"

"This is fantastic, Roya, thanks again and thanks in advance for whatever comes of this, what you're doing is terrific. Today is my first RDO."

"What's that? Your RDO?"

"Sorry, that's regular day off, the first of my two days off this week, but in light of all this new info, it looks like I'll be doing some work on my own time over the next couple days."

"Will the city pay you for that?"

"No, and actually, with what we're getting into, I would never let them know I was working anyway."

Chapter Fourteen

After Tommy returned home with Roya and JoJo, he showered and dressed for the day. He sat on the edge of his bed in his mother's apartment and sent a text to Lisa Yan. "Think we could meet up this morning at the Orion again?"

In less than two minutes, "Sure, what time?"

"Any time, it's my RDO, make it work for you, earlier will be better though."

"Okay, 9:00 AM?"

"Done deal, see you there."

Tommy then took a breath, paused for a minute as he thought and decided something, then punched another text into his phone, this one to the journalist who had covered both the Sister Margaret, and Hayden Jon Marshall cases, "Hey Gil, how you doing? You free for lunch today?"

Tommy sat for a couple of minutes, then laid down in his bed, JoJo lying next to him and resting his head on Tommy's stomach. Ten minutes passed and his phone buzzed.

"Detective Keane! Yes, I am! Tell me when and where and I'll be there!"

"How about noon, and we'll meet back at the Globe, you remember the place, yes?"

"Noon is perfect, and yes of course."

"Very good, I'll see you there."

"I'm intrigued!"

***

8:54 AM The Orion Diner.

Tommy arrived and was again happy to see Lisa Yan sitting and waiting for him in the same spot she was the last time they met. He slipped into the booth across from her.

"Good morning, Tom."

"Hey Lisa, how you doing?"

"Doing well. I'm curious, actually very curious, as to what you want to share with me this morning?"

Before Tommy could reply, the waitress approached so he paused, "Good morning, can I get you something to drink?"

"Yes, I'll have a coffee, with half and half please, and I'm ready to order if you are, Tommy?"

"Sure, go ahead."

"I'll have a spinach, tomato, and Swiss omelet please, and a small glass of orange juice as well."

"And for you, sir?"

"I'll have a bacon, egg, and cheese on a roll, and an unsweetened iced tea, please."

"Okay, got it! I'll have that right out for you."

"Alright, so why have I called you here to this lovely diner, again? Well, Lisa, I have a CI who has come across a massive amount of information concerning the Woos, and all sorts of nefarious activities that they are up to."

"Really?" Lisa was visibly excited and leaned forward.

"Yes. The 'but', however, is how and where this information was obtained. It's most likely, and probably a little less than kosher, and using it... well, if we were to use it, we would have to be extremely clever and careful not to jam ourselves up. This evidence may be, what they say, "Fruit of the poisonous tree," and I certainly wouldn't want it to hurt either of our careers or jeopardize the wellbeing of my CI."

"Okay, I, I understand, so let me ask you now... What does your CI have? How much do you trust him? And how would you suggest we work with him and the information?"

"Well, he says," Tommy continued with Lisa's 'him' reference, as it immediately added an additional thin layer of protection and concealment to Roya. Lisa's automatic assumption that she was a male, in his mind, would possibly help her anonymity if only in a minute manner. "He's got hundreds, possibly thousands, of pages of emails and text messages between Mama Woo, and other gang members discussing the Woo's family business."

"Really – Wow! I, I mean wow, how was he able to? ..."

"I have no idea, when it comes to this tech stuff. I am a complete and utter dinosaur, but from what I understand it is a truly massive amount of data, and how much do I trust this guy? Well, all I can say is that he has always come through for me. I would not only trust the information and wherever it came from to be wholly accurate, but over time, I have come to trust him as a truly decent and good-hearted individual, who wants nothing more than to do the right thing."

"This all sounds pretty positive, why…"

"Why get you involved?"

"Yes, as curious as I am, and as much as I want to see the Woos prosecuted and brought to justice, why share this with me?"

"Simple. I need you, Lisa. This information, this massive amount of information my CI has uncovered, is all in Chinese. And so far, it can't be translated via any program he has used, sure there are bits and pieces, but overall, it's unreadable. We think it may be written in some gangland slang or code, or simply an unusual dialect that the programs can't translate – I know you are gifted in the language department. I also know you probably know more about the Woos, and the Purple Dragons, than anyone else in the department. Also, I'm sure you realize, my dealings or at least my case dealing with Mama Woo, is basically closed. And for me to open an investigation into all the Woo's illegal enterprises would certainly be met with resistance."

"Yes, yes, I see…"

"Also, I think you're on the level. I think I can trust you to run with this information, to be thorough and methodical in your approach to this investigation, and you sit in the perfect and very credible position to receive some anonymous information from a concerned citizen... My thought is just that, my CI will give you everything he has come across anonymously, you are currently tied to nothing, and never will be. You can follow these leads wherever they may take you, do with them as you see fit. I am only here as an introductory member of the team. My CI will remain anonymous to you, and if the information is fruitful, well you Lisa, just may be the one to bring all the Woos, Purple Dragons, and possibly dozens of their associates to justice."

Lisa sat back in the booth. She was a bit astonished at what Tommy had just told her, and quickly processed the possibilities, and the answers this information may hold.

"Count me in."

"You're sure? That was an awful quick answer."

"One hundred and ten percent! I'm in. My whole life I've watched what the Woos, and people like the Woos, have done to my people and our communities. If I have the chance to bring some of them, any of them, to justice I will, and Tommy..."

Lisa paused, and took a breath to help keep her composure, "Thank you, thank you so much for having the confidence to share this with me. I think, I think you are an honorable man, and the fact that you are placing this confidence in me, honors me. I will not take that for granted, I will do my best to bring the Woos down, you have my word on that."

As Lisa finished, the waitress came and sat their orders in front of them, the conversation continued as they began to eat.

"Okay then, you can expect a thumb drive to arrive at your office in the next day or two. It will arrive by mail from an anonymous source, save the package it comes in… just in case anyone ever questions your source you'll have physical evidence available. I know I don't have to say this, but I will anyway – trust no one, Lisa, we know this case runs deep. You and I will never speak of this via phone or any sort of messaging again." Tommy paused and took a sip of his iced tea. "I think we both have concerns with the FBI's interest and involvement, and I think there may also be a leak within the DA's office. Somehow Min's location was compromised and four men, two of them ID'd as Marty and Tony Chu, paid a visit to the hotel she was lodged in…"

"Oh no! Is she okay?"

"She's fine, luckily. She was out grabbing some food when they showed up and kicked the door to her room open -- the brazen bastards. She got back to find the broken door and ran. I stashed her away in another hotel and only I know where she is, she's safe for now."

"Yes, I know all too well, just how deep this case is, I have many, many, suspicions. Things in fact that I won't share with you right now because I think it's better that I hold these suspicions as close to my chest as I can, until I have more evidence. And God willing, this CI of yours may just have the key to everything I have been working on for the last couple of years."

***

11:52 AM The Globe 158 East 23rd Street.

Tommy arrived at the Globe to find it hadn't opened yet, as it didn't open until noon, so he waited. Within a few minutes he heard the lock on the door tumble from inside and a tall, thin, cheerful man, with an Irish brogue, opened the door, "If yer waitin' on us man, we're open, come on in!"

"Thanks pal, good to see you," Tommy said as he made his way to the bar and took a seat.

"What'll it be, me friend?" The same gentleman asked, this time from behind the bar.

"Bottle of Bud, please."

At 12:04, Gil Nunez arrived to find Tommy waiting for him. Tommy stood, and they shook hands and exchanged pleasantries, then moved from the bar to one of the booths across from the bar. The place was currently empty and very private but for the staff.

"You have me very interested, Detective Keane. I've been so curious about this meeting all day, what? What have you got for me this time?"

"Menu Gents?" A young Irish woman of about twenty-five interjected.

"Please," Tommy replied. "I'll take another Bud, please, and what would you like, Gil?"

"I'll just have a seltzer with lemon, thanks."

As the waitress left, Tommy began, "I have a favor to ask Gil, I'm looking for... Well, I'm looking to put some heat on a case, although my involvement in this case is over ..."

And Tommy went on to tell the story of Li Jun, her miserable life, and how it all ended for her. Gil listened intently as Tommy spoke, pausing only when they placed their lunch orders, fish and chips for Tommy and a cheesesteak for Gil, and then once again as their food was delivered.

"So really you see, my involvement with Li Jun, and the Woos is pretty much over, or so it would seem. But I have come across a large amount of very damning information. I can't share the source of this information unfortunately, but as it becomes translated and more comes to light, I would like to hand some of it over to you. I'll be selective, these are very serious and very dangerous people, and they have some deep underworld connections and I think quite possibly some national and international political connections as well."

"This sounds like some heavy stuff, please go on."

"Well, much of it again is still unknown. What I can tell you is that these people are mixed up in millions, possibly billions of dollars' worth of human and drug trafficking. I have suspicions of possible involvement with federal agencies, as well as some here in the courts system. I can't prove shit right now, but as I get this information what I'd like for you to do is possibly a series of stories. Stories that will bring some heavy heat down on these murderous savages, something that will hopefully help bury this organization, and maybe help weed out some corruption and moreover force these cowardly judges to hammer these vicious gangsters whenever they eventually end up in a court of law."

"I love it. I am familiar with the Woos. I remember the Chinatown killings during the war with the Ha Sing Tong, the Woo's are serious business. So yes. Yes, I will absolutely do some stories on this, maybe use the Li Jun murder as an introduction. Explain how no one cares about these underground flesh peddlers, and everything I can dig up about these young women. Then move into the narcotics trafficking that goes with it, then the murder and finally the corruption. I'm certain the editor will love this once I pitch it to him, if we can dig deep enough, I may be able to get a couple stories out a week and have it last for weeks as long as your information is good and keeps bearing fruit, yes, yes this could be a great story, Detective Keane."

"Great, I am glad you're interested in taking it on, and please call me by my first name."

"Of course, Tommy, and let me thank you once again for working with me and handing me yet another tremendous story. I promise I will do right by you, and, and right by Li Jun.

***

As Tommy worked his angles with Lisa Yan and Gil Nunez, more and more chatter was coming through and being picked up by the computers and cell phones Roya had monitoring the Woos, and the Purple Dragons. As she would pour over it, she found that only slightly more than ten percent of it was discernible via her translation programs, and sadly was unable to find any better tool to use.

She was, however, able to begin to pick up patterns and identify various devices used in these conversations and threads. She was unable to attach them to individuals yet, but slowly there came to be more reason to this twisted riddle, and she hoped things would soon begin to make some sort of sense.

Around 3:00 PM, Roya received a message from Tommy, "A walk today when you get home?"

"I'm home." Was her reply.

"I'll hit you up soon."

At about 3:50 Tommy hit the corner of 88th and 2nd Avenue and texted Roya as he did, "I'll be downstairs in two minutes if you're ready for that walk?"

"Bet I beat you to the stoop!" Was Roya's reply.

And she was right, Tommy had no interest in running down the block and saw Roya step out of the building as he approached.

"Ha!" She yelled, "I told you I'd beat you!"

"Yeah, you beat me alright, I wasn't about to run just to make it here first." Tommy laughed.

"That's cause you're old and no fun!"

"I think you got me on both counts there, kid, come take a walk with me, and tell me what you've been able to get on our gangland friends so far."

The two began walking towards 1st Avenue at a rather slow and comfortable pace.

Roya began, "Okay, so I came home a little early today because I'm really interested in seeing what I can get for you on these people, and, well it's good and it's not so good news – the good is that all of my clones and hacks are working beautifully, I have just literally so much information coming in, both old stuff and new messages and emails as well. I have also been collecting new email and IP addresses from several different individual accounts, and this, well this is amazing news, because it is just so, so much information."

"But?"

"Well, the 'but' is what I had mentioned this morning, it's almost all unreadable by my programs. I have an algorithm that is finding patterns and may help us break a code if one exists. But language wise, I've only been able to decipher maybe ten percent of what I've caught. And of that, there are only a few actual sentences here and there that come through, – But it's only been a day, hopefully with some time more will come to light."

"Alright, well I really like the good news, hopefully all of this information will pan out to be something awesome, and as far as your bad news, I think I may have a way around it -- what I'll need from you is a thumb drive of everything you've got so far, and please make sure there is no way for some techy geek like yourself to ever trace anything back to you, that is really important..."

Roya stopped walking and stared at Tommy with a sarcastic look on her face. "Who you think you're talking to? Way to trace anything back? Listen, in this world I am the queen of the jungle alright, and anonymity is the game, so no, nothing will be traceable, and I can give you a high-capacity flash drive today, no problem. May have to give you a couple today, there is a lot of information coming through."

"Don't get smart, young lady. I know you know this is some serious shit we're getting into. I have to know you're safe, and gonna stay safe."

"I understand, now how may I ask, are you going to translate this? I assume you have another person you're going to pass this onto that you think may be able to break the code... Some sort of military thing? Or maybe a linguist who will be able to translate uncommon Chinese dialects?"

"I got someone."

"That's it? I got someone?"

"Trust me, the less you know the safer you are. Everyone involved will only know what it is that they are doing. No one will ever have a clue about anyone else, or their role in what we're doing."

"So, this shit is really deep then, huh?"

"I have a feeling it is, Roya, I really have no idea just how deep, but just be as careful as you can. These people are very dangerous and from what I understand are part of an international organization with some very lethal and powerful connections."

Roya stopped again, "Okay then, let's head back, I'll fill those flash drives for you, and you can get them to whoever your polyglot friend is?"

"Polyglot, what the fuck is a polyglot?"

Roya giggled, "Should I make you look it up?"

"Let me guess? Someone who speaks several languages?"

"Correct! Sherlock Holmes, has nothing on you and your powers of deduction does he, Detective Keane?"

"Feeling a little sassy today aren't you, Roya?"

"C'mon man, I'm sassy every day."

***

Tommy and Roya headed home; Tommy to his mother's apartment, where he found Maria, in her recliner watching television and smoking a cigarette, and Roya ran up to her apartment and filled four flash drives. Two originals and two copies for Tommy. Once she was done, she texted Tommy to meet her in the hallway, where she handed them off in two separate plain paper envelopes explaining how each contained the same information, and how one was for him, so he'd have a backup copy.

"Thanks again, Roya."

"I'll have more for you tomorrow or the next day. A lot of these are older messages, just a few new ones, but the more I break these open the more stuff I'm receiving in real time, I'll keep you posted."

"You are the goods kid! Let's hope my polyglot can read these."

Roya smiled at Tommy, and although they joked, there was a look in her eyes, one of admiration, respect, and gratitude for him. Not only for reaching out to her again, but in having enough confidence in her that he did. She knew Tommy's world was a serious and dangerous place, but she couldn't help but be excited to once again be helping him out, and knowing her contributions mattered, really mattered in real people's lives. Her smile was followed by a wink, "Goodnight, Tommy."

Tommy smiled back acknowledging the look in her eye's, and in a lower, almost paternal voice simply replied, "Goodnight, sweet girl."

***

Tommy let himself back into his mother's apartment, and was met by a very eager JoJo, who jumped and jumped until Tommy picked him up and gave him some kisses.

"Hiya, Tommy, what are you doing tonight, Tommy? You heading back out tonight, Tommy?

"No, I was hoping to stay in and watch a little TV right here with you, if that's alright, Ma?"

"Oh yes, Tommy! Yes, I would love that, Tommy, what would you like to watch? Are you hungry, Tommy? Can I fix you something, Tommy?

"You know what, Ma? I would love that. How about you grill me up one, no make it two of your famous grilled cheese sandwiches, and we'll see what TCM has playing tonight, I bet we can find something good on there."

Tommy was happy with what he had gotten done on what was the first of that week's RDOs, and he felt relaxed, and at home. He and his mother sat and laughed as they watched the movie Fatso, from 1980 starring Dom Deloise and Anne Bancroft, on TCM. Little JoJo sat on his lap eagerly waiting for Tommy to hand over bits of the crust from each of the grilled cheese sandwiches his mother had made him.

Li Jun

Chapter Fifteen

Tommy's eyes opened to the darkness of his room at his mother's apartment. He reached for his phone which read 7:12 AM. 'Nice' he thought. His productive day, and relaxing evening spent with his mother and dog, had been topped off with just over nine hours of solid sleep, and he felt good about whatever this day, his second day off, would hold for him.

As he lay his phone back on the nightstand, little JoJo inched his way closer and kissed Tommy on the side of his head, Tommy responded by giving a scratch to the dog's head and ear. He then rolled off the bed and banged out his fifty morning pushups, then stood, pulled on some sweatpants, a sweatshirt, some sneakers, and his leather car coat. He gave JoJo a whistle and a nod to join him as he stuffed his .38 revolver in his coat pocket and headed to the door for the first walk of the day.

The two of them stepped out onto the stoop and both looked to the left, then to the right, as they scanned the block. They then stepped off the stoop and began their walk over to Glaser's Bake Shop, where Tommy got a tea and an apple turnover for himself, and a coffee and three black and white cookies for his mother, who, upon Tommy returning home, thanked him for the cookies but then had to ask why he would buy her a coffee when she could make herself one at home?

Tommy then showered and dressed for the day. Although it was his day off, he had some things to take care of regarding the Woos; the first was to check on Min, make sure she was safe, comfortable, and fed, the second was to mail Roya's flash drives to Lisa Yan. Tommy had decided it would be best to do this from the post office on West 38th Street, over by where he had lodged Min. His thought was in the event anyone was ever to look into where this anonymous information had come from, it would be traced back to a post office neighborhood away from where Tommy and Roya lived, as well as precincts away from the 2-1, adding an additional layer of anonymity.

Finally, his last task of the day was to get with Molly. She had messaged him several times over the last few days, and although Tommy had answered her messages, he felt he had been too short with her, with answers like, "Can't now I'm working." "Hit you back later." And "Not now." Answers he knew in retrospect were unnecessarily short, somewhat rude, and simply unfair. He was already messaging her, why couldn't he simply add an explanation, and maybe something kind, or sweet?

Fact was, when Tommy was in the thick of a serious investigation, and his mind locked in on a case, almost everything else became an afterthought. It was this focus that made him an outstanding detective, but it was a quality that also hurt his relationships, and no doubt contributed to the divorce of his beloved Cookie.

***

The morning went smoothly. He dropped the package off at the Post Office. Min was very happy to see Tommy, he escorted her out of the hotel and took her for some pizza at Capizzi on 9th Avenue. He then again stocked her up with snacks and drinks and promised to return the following day.

He then messaged Molly, "Hey Molly, how you doing? Sorry I've been off the grid all week, had a serious case I was dealing with, that's absolutely no excuse though, and I apologize for putting you off, that was wrong of me, and unfair to you."

A few minutes passed as he walked east on 37th Street when his phone buzzed with a message from Molly, "Hey handsome stranger! I was wondering when I was going to hear from you again."

"I'm sorry Molly, I truly am, I was just up to my neck in it this week."

"It's cool, I appreciate the apology, but a girl has to expect this if she wants to date a crime fighter!"

"You're sweet to understand, but you deserved more from me than just a bunch of two- and three-word replies, and I am sorry."

"Apology accepted! (smiley face emoji) I'm at work, you wanna come by or meet up later today?"

"I would, yes."

"K, check ya lata"

***

Bailey's was hopping. There was a good after-work crowd filing in, and Molly, who looked as cute as ever in her tight jeans and tiny t-shirt, smiled when her eyes met Tommy's. She held up one finger as if to say 'Just a minute' as she quickly served a trio of patrons who sat midway down the bar.

Tommy's favorite stool was taken, but he was happy to find one available a quarter of the way down the bar and took his coat off and hung it on the back of the chair. Before he could sit, Molly, now on the patron's side of the bar, ran towards him as if she hadn't seen him in years. She jumped up onto him, wrapping her legs around his waist and her arms around his neck, forcefully pulling their mouths together for a passionate kiss.

"Woo Hoo!" Was heard from someone in the crowd as Molly kissed Tommy again and again all over his face.

"I missed you, missed you, missed you, my handsome man!" Tommy enjoyed this energetic greeting, which immediately cheered him up, something he needed.

Molly headed back behind the bar, and promptly sat a bottle of Budweiser and a rocks glass of Jameson in front of him.

"So happy to see you." She said as she turned to take care of more customers.

Gerry Nealey, AKA 'Old Man Nealey,' smiled at Tommy with his unshaven face, and three missing teeth, "Now that's what I call service, son!"

"I have no idea who that woman is!" Tommy replied, rather loudly, getting a laugh from his corner of the bar.

Tommy drank a couple more beers and cajoled with Gerry, and a few of the other old timers, sharing stories and jokes. Molly's shift came to an end, and she joined everyone at the end of the bar for one last shot and a beer.

"Where you wanna go for dinner tonight? Italian, maybe some Thai? I don't care, whatever you like, I'm up for anything."

"I haven't seen you all week, Tommy, I think we pick up some Chinese from Charley Mom, head over to my place, get naked, and you eat fried rice and dumplings off my belly?"

A united "Whoa!" erupted from the old timers that surrounded them and Gerry Nealey slapped Tommy so hard on his back that a bit of beer popped out of the bottle Tommy was holding in his hand.

Tommy smiled, slightly shocked and a little embarrassed, "How the fuck could anyone say no to that?" He answered loudly with a broad smile. They slid off their bar stools and shook the old timer's hands and said their goodbyes to the group that surrounded them. They both put their jackets on and headed out the door.

Tommy and Molly did get Chinese food from the Charley Mom restaurant on York Avenue and Molly did indeed have Tommy eat fried rice and dumplings off her lovely naked belly.

***

Molly got up from the bed, Tommy's eyes taking in her loveliness, "Can I get you a beer, or something?"

"A water please, I would love some water." As Tommy spoke, his phone went off. It was Mark Stein.

Molly froze in the doorway as she watched Tommy answer, curious if something was going to ruin this beautiful evening.

"Hey, Mark, what's up, all cool?"

Mark replied, almost singing the following, "Guess who's out of a co-oma?"

"Really? So? So, what do you know?"

"Nothing yet, I just called the Duty Captain, I'm headed up now, gonna sign in and go interview him. Thought maybe I'd tag you in for a little overtime, if you were interested, tell them you were pertinent to the investigation."

Tommy looked across the room and into Molly's beautiful green eyes, "Sorry, Mark, I'm kinda into something already tonight, but thanks for the heads up, and the offer. I am curious to know what happens so hit me up later, alright?"

As he finished the call, he kept his eyes locked with Molly. She quickly ran and leapt back into the bed, and straddled him, snatching his phone from his hand and throwing it across the room. She then grabbed and pinned his wrists to the bed.

"Kinda into something? Kinda into something?" She repeated with a devilish smile, her green eyes sparkling with excitement, "You're definitely gonna be getting back into something, and right now you sexy beast!"

Chapter Sixteen

Tommy woke up, rather late for him, on this his first day back to work after his two RDO's. He quietly got up and retrieved his phone from the floor, where Molly had tossed it a few hours prior, it was almost 9:00 AM. He had enjoyed a very sound night's sleep after a very satisfying evening spent with Molly.

He opened his phone to read the one text he had received while he slept from Mark Stein, "Did the interview, you're not going to believe what this guy told me, fill you in tomorrow when I see you."

'Not going to believe? -- What does that mean?' Tommy thought to himself, 'God, I hope it's not Terry and Gusty, those stupid bastards.'

Personally, he believed it was them, in fact he knew it had to be, the descriptions given by Miss Daniels were spot on. He knew the relationship between Macca, Terry, and Gusty, it was very simple arithmetic, and it all added up and pointed straight to Terry. That's why Mark had pulled those photos and Tommy knew he would have immediately done the same. He pursed his lips and cocked his head in fear of the possible upcoming arrest of his lifelong friend.

Molly murmured softly from the bed, "What's wrong lover? You look like you got some bad news there?"

"No, nothing bad, not yet anyway. Just a text from my partner about a case he's working on."

"Oh, stop with that shop talk, you have a few more hours before you need to go chase bad guys. How 'bout you come back to bed for a little while longer, then we'll take a shower together and I send you back to the front, all clean and shiny, relaxed, and full of love… Just in case you decide not to see me for a whole week again?"

Tommy slowly walked back across the room and got into Molly's bed. Lying next to her, his left hand propping up his head, while his right arm embraced her body.

"Molly, you sweet thing… I hate to say it, but I… I don't think this relationship of ours can continue, I… I absolutely love everything about you kid, but, well, let's face it, you're way too young for me, and, and, well there's just no future in us, you need a fella closer to your own age, and…"

Molly turned herself around, still in Tommy's embrace but now she was facing him and looking up at him from her pillow, his head still propped up on his elbow. She gently put her left index finger up to his mouth to silence him.

"Oh, you silly, man," she said softly, "I know this. Our relationship isn't getting serious. Don't worry about that. I know you are too old for me, and I'm not falling, and have no intentions of falling in love with you. I, well… I've just wanted you here in my bed, like this, probably since the first time I saw you walk into Bailey's. You're the most dead sexy man I have ever met Tommy, but no, no, I don't see or dream of a future with you, I just want to have what we have now. I like you a lot, but, well, you're more of an adventure for me, I don't, can't, see a future with you. Just some more good times like last night, I mean, we've had some good times, haven't we?"

Tommy paused to take her statement in, "I would say amazing times." He answered.

She smiled up at him, "I agree," she placed her index finger on his lips to silence him once more, "Now, no more talk. Let's get sexy one more time, then I'll shower you up, slap you on the ass, and send you off to work for the day."

***

Tommy arrived at the precinct about twenty minutes before his shift. As he made his way to the stairs leading up to the squad room, he heard Captain Pileggi's voice. "Detective Keane, a moment."

Tommy stopped, turned, and acknowledged the Captain. He walked back down the few steps and met him in front of the desk, where Sergeant Ruffolo sat staring down at his logbook, pretending he wasn't aware of the Captain and Tommy conversing just a few feet in front of him.

"Yes, Captain, what can I do for you?"

"I wanted to ask you about this murder investigation of the Asian prostitute. I'm curious why, Detective, you would be wantonly uncooperative with the FBI on this?"

Tommy took a moment before speaking as to not say the wrong thing, "Uncooperative, Captain?" he asked.

"Yes, that's what I said, Detective, I received a call from Agent Kai, and another from her supervisor, saying that they had asked to fold your case in with an ongoing case of theirs on this Woo organization, and that you were uncooperative. You withheld information that they felt may have been helpful and pertinent to their investigation. Why, Detective Keane, would you choose to be uncooperative with the FBI concerning a dead prostitute?"

Tommy again paused, "Well, Captain, it's very simple. This case, as you know, was closed by arrest just hours after it happened. The FBI, as I am sure you also know, has no jurisdiction when it comes to homicides. That, as always, falls to us, us, as in those of us in the Detective Squad who work these investigations. Now I did make it very clear to Agent Kai, and her partner, that they could get with the ADA handling the case down at the DA's office, and they would share anything they wanted with the FBI."

"Yes," Captain Pileggi then paused, he knew Tommy was right, "I just don't understand why you would intentionally be difficult with an agency like the FBI, Detective. We at the NYPD, and here at the 2-1, enjoy a good relationship with them and I found your attitude towards Agent Kai to be rather unprofessional. We do, after all, just want the same thing in the end, do we not? Justice brought to the unjust?"

"I guess you're right, Captain, it was a really long night, and I guess Agent Kai just rubbed me the wrong way."

Captain Pileggi, feeling he had somehow bettered Tommy in this exchange, took a step back and added, "Alright,

Detective, just please be more cognitive of this in the future. We don't want to be burning any bridges with the FBI. We may need their assistance sometime in the future."

As Captain Pileggi turned back towards his office, Tommy spoke out again,

"Yes, sir, and if I may … As you may or may not know, our witness in this case was almost murdered in her hotel room a couple of nights ago. I closed this case, but believe it still has legs. I also believe there is something bubbling under the surface, something neither you nor I are aware of. Something ugly, and with teeth… The kind of teeth that will bite anyone who gets too close to it. Now, as far as I'm concerned, outside of serving an arrest warrant I have been tasked with, on two men the District Attorney's office wants brought in for questioning, this is a closed case. The fact that the FBI wants in on it, tells me I want out, and respectfully Captain, I would suggest you stay as far away from the FBI, and anything involving the Woos as well, I think no good can come of it, no good at all."

"Are you advising me, Detective?" Captain Pileggi placed his hands on his hips and furrowed his brow at Tommy.

"I'm just telling you what I think, Captain, there is a lot more to this than any of us imagine, and I am happy to again state, outside of scooping up these two fellas for the DA's office, as far as I'm concerned this case is closed."

Tommy then turned and headed back to the staircase. Pileggi stood silently, not sure what to make of their brief conversation, but somehow felt unsatisfied, and curious about what Tommy knew and what he meant by this case still has legs and teeth.

***

Tommy passed Charice, and chatted for a moment commenting on her blouse, and how it matched the beads in her hair, then entered the squad room to find Jimmy, Doreen and Mark all sitting at their respective desks.

"Hey, Tommy, how were your RDOs?"

"Fine, D, yours?"

"Grand, just grand thanks, did nothing. Slept and read for two days straight with no interruptions, they were heaven!"

"Good for you. Jimmy, Mark," Tommy said turning his attention to the other two detectives.

"How you doin', Tommy?" Was Jimmy's reply.

"Afternoon, Tom." Mark commented, never taking his eyes up from the paper he was reading.

"So, I'm curious, Mark. What happened with Macca, did he ID anyone?"

"Oh yeah," Mark began, dropping the newspaper to his desk, "So let me tell you what happened there. I get the call that Macca is out of his coma, right? and I make my way over to the hospital. Now I know Macca, from a few years ago, and he remembers me as soon as I walk in the room, 'Good to see you, Stein.' He says right away, right. So I know, I know his mind is in good working order, so I get right into it and I ask him how he's feeling. Tell him what a tough fuck he is to survive this beating, do my best to butter him up a little and make him feel I'm on his side as much as I can, right?"

Mark took a breath while the rest of the squad listened intently.

"So, I continue, and ask him outright, do you know who did this to you, Joey?"

"I have a good idea, yes."

"Great, he knows who did this to him, so I tell him I have a few six packs to show him, and I put them one at a time on his hospital bed table, so he can look down on them, he stares at the first one for like ten seconds."

"Nope."

"Then the second one, again for like ten seconds."

"Nope, none of these guys either."

"So, I lay the third set of photos down. And again, he stares at them, studying them for at least ten seconds."

"Nope, none of these guys either."

"Now, I thought for sure two of these guys he would hit on, I kinda knew it, but it's a no on all three arrays. So, I ask him, you think you know who did this to you, and you're sure it's none of these guys?"

"No, these guys are all white, and it wasn't no white guy."

"So, it was a big black guy that did this to you?"

"Nope, was a big Dominican. Big strong guy, way over six feet, built like a truck."

"Really… And you think you know him?"

"Sure, I do."

"You got a name for me, Joey?"

"Yeah, it's… It's Julio, or Jose, maybe, maybe Juan, something like that, and it's Ramirez, or Suarez, or Melendez. I think… his first name starts with a J and his last name ends with a Z. And he's like six foot, maybe six foot six, or so, and big, like 225, maybe 265, something like that. For sure Dominican, but maybe Puerto Rican, or even Cuban, really, I couldn't tell you, I don't know him very well… But if you can bring me some pictures of some Dominican, Puerto Rican, Cubans, between six foot and six foot six, that weigh 225 – 265 pounds, with light-ish to darkish brown skin. I'll be happy to look at them for you, Stein. Anything to help catch the fuck that put me here, you know that Detective!"

Jimmy stared up at Mark, not quite getting it.

"Ha! That little fucker, he's D&D as well, huh?" Tommy replied.

"D&D?" Asked Jimmy.

"Yeah, D&D… Deaf and Dumb, you know, the old, 'I didn't see anything and I'm not saying anything.' He knows exactly who did this to him, and I'm sure I do too, but if he's not moving forward with this investigation and not being honest with me, I'm going to have to close it as an uncooperative victim. I'm curious to see if he's going to try and deal with this himself?" Mark answered.

Tommy stayed silent, but thought to himself, 'He wouldn't dare.' Then spoke up, changing the subject.

"So, listen up, I may need all of you in the next day or two to go grab a couple of guys on a warrant I have from the DA's office on two of the four men who tried to get at our witness in the Woo case the other night."

"Of course, Tommy." Said Doreen.

"Yeah, anything man." Said Jimmy

"How is our girl, Min?" Asked Mark.

"She seems surprisingly well. I'm going to check on her in a bit, but overall, she's doing well. She was a little shook up, but I think she is enjoying the first taste of freedom she has ever known, even if it is being all alone in a hotel room eating pizza and take out. But it's been a full week today, probably the first week since she is eleven, she hasn't had some filthy John on top of her."

"Oh my god what a horrible thought." Doreen added.

"I, I can't imagine what these poor girls have endured." Tommy replied. "But yeah, so as soon as I can get locations on these two hard case brothers, we'll go serve these warrants and scoop them up."

"Would you like me to do a search for you, Tommy?"

"Work a little sweet D magic for me? You know I would love that!" Tommy grinned at her.

"You got it, what are their names?"

"Marty and Tony Chu, and they're twins, no idea where they live, gonna guess here in Chinatown, or maybe in Flushing, but could be out in Brooklyn somewhere too?"

Li Jun

"I'll find em!"

***

As the squad's day continued within the confines of the 2-1, Lisa Yan received and opened an anonymous package that was delivered to her office in lower Manhattan. As she held the flash drives in her hands, she wanted to plug them into her computer right away but paused and went to the locker room to retrieve her personal laptop. There, in the privacy of the empty locker room, she plugged in one of the drives and within seconds was absolutely amazed at the amount of information she was able to see.

It took her only minutes to see how the Woos, and Purple Dragons, were messaging one another in a combination of a bastardized version of the Sanming dialect, and Hokkien. This mix, along with the heavy use of slang, would make it difficult for any computer program to translate. It was, at first, very difficult for Lisa to make sense of most of what she saw, but within an hour she began to see how these languages were being combined and used. She then had no difficulty reading and understanding the majority of what was in front of her.

She sat and read, and read, and read. Amazed at the mountain of information she had just received, she quickly realized that this treasure trove would take weeks, if not months, to unravel. She did, however, also realize this would be the end to many of the gangs and gangsters she had been attempting to track and investigate for the last few years. Just like that, boom, a careers worth of work sat on her lap, awaiting to be downloaded and investigated.

***

About thirty blocks north of Lisa Yan, a young Gil Nunez, was pitching a story to his editor. The story of a young sex worker flung out of a window to be impaled of some fence spikes below. An awful tale of a young woman sold to sex slavers as a child in a foreign land and trafficked to the United States where she was regularly raped, beaten, tortured, and deprived of every human dignity. This child, Li, was to be the face of the unknown tens of thousands living this life here in North America and one of millions worldwide.

Gil's pitch was so moving, it brought a tear to the hardened editor's eye, who immediately agreed to a multi piece expose. The stories would appear every other day, until they felt the story had run its course. The beginning would start with the death of Li Jun and her short history, following with the snakeheads who brought her here to United States, the Woos, and the Purple Dragons, who trafficked people and drugs indiscriminately, and the apparent disregard for it all, by both the government and the public at large.

***

Tommy banged out some reports for a few of his current open cases, then made his way down to the hotel he had Min lodged in. He took her out for lunch and to stock up on some food and toiletries for her room. He did his best to explain that this would be her life for a while and it would take some time before the District Attorney's office was able to move her to a better home, and even longer before the case would go to trial. The whole time he continued to reassure her she was safe and that he had her best interests at heart.

She understood what Tommy was telling her and at the end of the day's meeting, she thanked him.

"Thank you, Detective Tommy, I never think I have another friend since I lose Li, I never think I know a good man, ever, but you, Detective Tommy, good man, and I thank you, I know you good and you care for Min, and I thank you."

Tommy put his hands on Mins shoulders, and she placed her hands on top of his as to understand that Tommy did indeed care, and that Min was indeed safe now. He raised his left hand and with his thumb gently wiped a single tear away from her cheek. He promised to be in contact again soon and apologized, and explained, he had work to do and couldn't spend more time with her.

She nodded and thanked him again, then closed and locked the door to her room.

***

The rest of Tommy's night was uneventful. He returned to the squad room, typed away at several of his cases and took a ride to assist Doreen with an assault on 96th and Lexington. After which they stopped at Papaya King on 86th and 3rd for a couple of franks. They returned to the precinct for a little more typing and to sign out for the end of tour. He returned home straight after work, to his mother's apartment on 88th Street, where he found her asleep in her recliner with the television on. He kissed her gently on the head, gently woke her and walked her to her bedroom, and tucked her in.

Tommy and little JoJo then made their way to Tommy's room for the night.

Li Jun

Chapter Seventeen

Tommy truly had no idea what he had set in motion. He knew Roya would come up with something but had no idea the volumes of information she would acquire. All day, and all night, her computers continued to gather old information as well as messages in real time.

He had hoped, and believed, Lisa Yan would be an asset to his cause, but had no idea just how strong her linguistic, and investigative, abilities were. Or how dedicated she would be to this case and to putting an end to the Woos, and the infamous Purple Dragons.

As Tommy and JoJo had retired that evening, Lisa was approaching her twelfth hour of reading and decoding hundreds of messages. She had become a woman possessed, the information was too intriguing; dates, names, locations, orders, deliveries, addresses - she couldn't have imagined this much evidence falling in her lap, and each piece of information just fueled her to read and search for more.

As all of this information gathering, and deciphering, was going on at different ends of the city, Gil Nunez filed his copy for the first of his multi-story expose on the death of Li Jun, and Chinese organized crime in New York City. He wrote to convey how its tentacles stretched around the world. From what he learned at his meeting with Tommy, what he was able to research online, as well as what he was able to learn from the papers data banks, Gil already thought he could do about five pieces on what was happening. He had a feeling he was just scratching the surface as to what would come.

***

Tommy's eyes opened to the darkness of his room and the weight of little JoJo's front paws on his chest, with one paw scratching to let Tommy know he wanted to go out.

He lifted the puppy up and set him to the side, then rolled out of bed and onto the floor in the darkness for his fifty morning pushups. He then stood and turned on his bedside lamp and checked his phone, it was 8:12 AM. He pulled on some sweats, threw on a jacket, stuffed his revolver into its pocket then headed out the door with JoJo.

They had a short walk then returned home. Tommy kissed his mother good morning, ate a little oatmeal, and sat on the sofa next to her. Maria was already watching television with a cup of coffee in one hand and a cigarette in the other.

As she cursed at the news, and complained about the mayor, Tommy nodded and agreed. He felt his phone go off and dug it out of his pocket. It was a text from Roya.

"I have something for you, are you available this morning?"

"Sure am, hallway? Now?" was his response.

"Sure."

Tommy stood and excused himself, "I'll be right back, Ma, hold that thought." He said, somewhat sarcastically. He headed out into the hallway and up the stairs to meet Roya. They met on the third floor, she sat down on the steps as Tommy stayed standing, and she began.

"We are getting a lot of information here, man, a ton of it's in real time. Slowly, I am able to put little bits and pieces together, but really, I am lost here as far as what any of it means. any word from you linguist person?"

"No, nothing yet. I'm not sure if he's even gotten his hands on your drives yet. But I hope to hear something today."

"Well, here you go, another load of info for him to dig into."

"Thanks, Roya, I really appreciate this, have an awesome day kid."

Roya smiled and winked.

"You have a good one too."

Tommy showered, shaved, and dressed for the day. He wanted to get out early so he could mail the new flash drive to Lisa, then go and check on Min, both of which would take him into the early afternoon. As he approached the entrance to the subway on 86th Street his phone went off, it was Lisa Yan,

"Hello?"

"Can I buy you lunch, sir?"

"Absolutely, same place?"

"No, we need something with a real bar for this one."

"Really? Well, okay then how about Foley's on West 33rd? I'll be in that neighborhood before I head in for tonight's tour, I haven't been there for a while. but they always had decent food."

"Sounds like a plan, one o'clock?"

"Done deal, I'll see you there."

"Okay, bye bye."

Tommy at first was happy about this meeting, thinking that meeting Lisa, would save him a trip to the post office to mail the new flash drives, but then he thought better of it. The trick to the anonymity of these drives was that they were showing up unannounced in her office by an unknown informant. He went right back to his original plan of mailing the drives from the post office, checking on Min, and then after that, meeting up with Lisa Yan at Foley's.

***

12:53 PM Foley's NY Pub & Restaurant 18 West 33rd Street.

Tommy entered Foley's and it was just as he had remembered it. Long and narrow, and covered in baseball memorabilia. Jerseys hung from the ceiling, display cases featured bobble heads and autographed baseballs. He was never much of a sports fan, but he did appreciate the effort the owners had gone through, to make the little gem of a pub a Shangri La for the baseball aficionado.

Tommy found that Lisa had once again arrived before he had and found her towards the rear of the pub waiting at a small table for two. As he approached her, she stood wearing a broad smile, she extended her tiny hand towards Tommy, who returned a smile and took her hand in his. She attempted her best to give him a strong, firm handshake with one vigorous up and down motion, then stated demurely.

"I have to give you a hug." Then leaned in wrapped her arms around him and squeezed as tightly as she could.

"Well, hello, Lisa. Something tells me you are happy today?" He asked coyly, knowing full well what she was happy about. As they both took their seats she immediately began.

"This informant of yours, has - has delivered the most amazing amount of information. Names, dates, and locations. We have gang members discussing crimes. Gossiping about one another. This is such an amazing get, I, I am absolutely blown away by what this guy has delivered."

"So, you are able to read it then?"

"It is difficult, but I'm getting through it."

"Is it coded or in a dialect that the computer programs can't pick up?"

"A little of both, actually, not so much coded, as just really slanged up. Most of the back and forth is written in the Sanming dialect, one that I am fluent in. However, they all seem to write to one another in a rough poor version of this dialect, as well as in Hokkien, which is another crude form of Chinese. I have heard it referred to as gangster talk, which is not accurate in my opinion, it's just a crude way to speak. I can see how programs, which are designed to translate proper Chinese to proper English, simply can't translate this stuff. I mean, look at how our own hood rats speak to each other here in New York, do you think any software would be able to translate any of that gibberish?"

"No, I see exactly what you're saying, and it makes perfect sense. So, you're happy then?"

"Oh my god, yes! I've been reading and translating nonstop! I already have deciphered them talking about what I believe are murders, deliveries of drugs and human beings, a price list of crimes - from simple threats and extortion, to what they call the Top Job, which I am certain means murder. It's going to take some doing but, oh my god, we are going to close so many cases, and lock up so many awful people with this. I just know it, this is going to be huge... Effing huge, Tommy!"

Tommy smiled at Lisa, and got a thrill from her enthusiasm, "Well best of luck, hopefully you'll be able to cut the heads off of one or two of these snakehead fuckers."

"That's the plan, and that's why I wanted to talk to you today. I have already put together a large proposal for my supervisor, on how we should disseminate all this information, and how I think we can approach this. It will be a ton of work but if I can put a team together with my office, and the DA's office, I think we'd could start building cases, and making arrests in a matter of weeks. And I'm talking serious arrests and serious numbers... Ahh! I am so excited... But I wanted to meet with you first, I wanted to thank you for this, and we need to have a drink to toast this for good luck. I'm going to buy you lunch and, well... then ask you if you have any advice for me?"

The waitress came by with menus and asked what they wanted to drink.

"Oh gee, what do you want? Should we have Champagne?"

"I'm not much of a Champagne fan, but this is your party, we'll do whatever you like, dear."

"No, no you're right, we're NYPD Detectives, let's have beer, and we'll do a shot for our toast! Name your poison, Detective!"

Tommy smiled at her; she was as excited as a schoolgirl on her way to prom. "I'll take a bottle of Bud, and a shot of Jameson, please."

"And for you?" The waitress asked Lisa.

"Hmm, I'll have something light on draft and I'll have a shot of Jameson too, please."

As the waitress left to fill their orders, Tommy asked, "So what advice do you need?"

"Well, I don't know to be honest. I just feel that this may be a lot to handle. I know what I want to do, but I'm not sure how to go about it. I know you have so much experience with all manner of crimes and arrests, and well, I guess I really want to know how not to screw this up?"

"Ahh, I see," Tommy leaned forward and placed his elbows on the table, "Well, I don't know right away what to tell you, but I will say this – I don't know you long, really, let's face it, I don't know you at all, Lisa, but I do believe you are a very smart person, probably a brilliant person. I also have a strong feeling that your heart is in the right place, believe me, if I didn't, I would have never approached you with this information…"

"Thank you." She replied in a less excited voice, a little surprised by Tommy's kind words.

"So, what I will say, or I guess give as advice is to simply be true. Be true to yourself, know that you are doing the right thing, take your time and be methodical with your investigation. Don't let the case load get to you, or any pressures from the brass, the DA's office, or the press get in the way of your judgement. This case, or these cases rather, are yours, you are the only one in the world in possession of this information. Own it… Fucking own it, Lisa."

Lisa took a huge deep breath, then rubbed her eyes, almost in disbelief, "This is going to be huge, isn't it?"

Tommy sat back in his chair.

"I think, if everything you have told me is correct, this is going to make your career. Just be cool, careful, and methodical. Make sure you hold this information as close to your chest as possible. We both know there are rats and vultures who are going to be all over this once it breaks, just be cool, Lisa, just be cool."

"Oh God, I am so excited. So, so excited, can I, is it okay to call on you if I have any questions?"

"Absolutely, anytime, but again, be cool, no emails no texts, just lunch." And he smiled that sincere Tommy smile at her.

The waitress returned with their drinks and took their food orders. Lisa requested the Poached Salmon and Tommy, the Shepard's Pie. Then came the toast.

"Pick up your glass, Detective Keane, this one is for you, and all you've done for me with your informant and this case."

"If I may, Lisa, let's do this shot for that dear sweet little Li Jun, may she rest in peace."

"You're right, to Li Jun."

"To Li Jun."

Li Jun

Chapter Eighteen

The two ate their lunch, finished their drinks, and got to know one another a little better, sharing family stories, and photos from their phones for an hour or so before they left the pub, and went their separate ways. Lisa went back to her office and Tommy back to the 2-1. He had a little time on his hands yet, so he decided to walk the two or so miles to the precinct.

As he made his way into the station house Sergeant Diaz, who was on the desk, nodded his head with a bit of a smirk, "Yo Keane, you made the papers again pal, big write up about that dead pro over on 80th Street last week. I don't know for sure, but I heard the captain mumbling something under his breath about it… Just a heads-up brother, that fucker may have a bug up his ass over it, reporter did a good job, dynamite story, gives you a little mention in the beginning. Good job man."

"Hey thanks, Sarge, and a bug up his ass? Our Captain Pileggi? Nahh, never." Tommy smiled and laughed with Sergeant Diaz, but as he headed up the stairs, he also took a deep breath and let out a sigh expecting to hear some kind of shit from the Captain that night, or in the very near future.

***

As Tommy entered the squad room to start his shift, Lisa Yan was sitting down with her sergeant and lieutenant downtown and began to explain about this bundle of anonymous information that had landed in her lap the day prior. She explained how she spent the entire night examining it, deciphering it, and vetting it, and told them how it all appeared to be wholly authentic. How she was able to verify and cross reference several organized crime members, along with some street gang members, as well as what she believed to be corroborating evidence pertaining to numerous cases the Asian Gang unit were already working on. Some which had gone cold.

Both her sergeant and her lieutenant were amazed at what Lisa had brought to the table and they all sat together for a little over three hours discussing how to proceed. All agreed that the best line of action would be to form a special task force within the unit with Lisa acting as lead investigator.

It was unknown to Lisa during this meeting that both her sergeant and lieutenant had just read, and were discussing, the Gil Nunez, article in the paper. They knew the heat would soon be coming down on them from the Chief of Detectives as to what they were doing to help stop sex trafficking in the city, so it could not have been a better day, or a better hour, for her to come to them with her pitch.

Back at the 2-1 Tommy entered the squad room, he was met by Detectives Keogh and Volpe from A Squad, and by Stein, who was sitting at his desk with an open briefcase picking out which of his two ties he would wear for this tour.

"Oh! Here he is! Detective Keane, man of the hour, kickin' ass and takin' names. Keane makes the paper once again!" Keogh sounded off in his loud barreling voice.

"What you talking about, Keogh?" Tommy asked.

"You got the paper there, Stein, read what they said about our man Tommy here!"

"Alright," Mark began as he picked up the paper, "What's it say here exactly? Pertaining to that young girl who was killed last week over on 80th, here is your part, you can read the whole article yourself, but your part goes like this Tom:

"THIS HOMICIDE HAPPENED IN THE 21ST PRECINCT, AND WAS ASSIGNED TO THE CITY'S FAVORITE INVESTIGATOR, DETECTIVE THOMAS KEANE. THE SAME DETECTIVE THIS REPORTER WROTE ABOUT LAST NOVEMBER, WHO WAS RESPONSIBLE FOR FREEING THE CHILDREN FROM THE CHILD ABDUCTING CULT ON EAST 82ND STREET, AND WHO WAS ALSO INSTRUMENTAL IN FINDING THE KILLER OF THE NOW DISGRACED NUN, SISTER MARGARET, LAST OCTOBER ON EAST 93RD STREET."

"Good job, Tom."

"The city's favorite investigator!" Volpe said in a childish voice, slightly singing it as he said it, "I know he's, my favorite! How bout you, Keogh? – Is he your favorite too?"

"Only on the mornings he brings bagels, or when he's buying the shots, other than that he's always number two to you sweet cheeks!"

"Here let me see that." Tommy asked Mark, then he sat and read the article as the three other men continued goofing around as they banged away on their keypads.

It was a nice long article, about three quarters of a page long, it described the death of Li Jun, and surmised in detail at what an awful life she must have had.

"THESE YOUNG WOMEN AND BOYS ARE RAPED BY MEN AS MANY AS TWENTY OR MORE TIMES A DAY," it called out Mama and Peter Woo, mentioned Teddy Lo, and the Purple Dragons, and reminded its readers of the war that had occurred between them and the Ha Sing Tong years prior where, "THE PURPLE DRAGONS, HUNG THE MUTILATED CORPSES OF THEIR RIVALS FROM FIRE ESCAPES,"

The article made a point to call out Chinese organized crime as a worldwide terror organization that was responsible for many more deaths per year than the Italian Mafia has committed in the entirety of its existence.

When Tommy was finished with the piece he handed the paper back to Mark, "Heavy article wasn't it?" Mark asked.

"Fuck yeah, hopefully some judges read it and remember it the next time a Purple Dragon sets foot in their courtroom."

As they continued discussing the article, Jimmy and Doreen walked into the squad room,

"Evening gents." Jimmy said.

"We heard you made the paper again, Tommy, something about that girl that was killed last week?" Doreen asked.

"Yeah, so you heard too! Our Keane here is 'The City's Favorite Investigator.' My vote was for you Doreen, but that

Nunez, we think he's got the hots for our Keane here." Keogh said, again in his sarcastic and booming voice.

"I haven't read it yet" Doreen continued, "but I know Tommy would be getting my vote! Especially on the mornings when he brings the bagels in!"

With that, Keogh, Volpe, Stein, and Tommy all let out a roar, Doreen not quite sure what she said exactly, but was happy it struck such a hilarious chord with this crew. Jimmy just looked at Doreen and shrugged, not being privy to what Keogh had just said minutes before.

***

About an hour into their tour, Doreen called Tommy over to her desk,

"Here, Tommy, I have two possible addresses for your Chu twins, both in Queens. Sounds like they are a couple of serious bad asses, huh?"

"No doubt, the two of them are definitely up to their necks in prostitution and drug dealing. I wouldn't be surprised if they have a few bodies under their belts as well, from what I understand they are ruthless enforcers for a multi-million dollar a year crime organization, and when I say multi, I'm talking hundreds of millions."

"I bet there are some bodies connected to these two. I see both have attempted murder arrests, numerous assaults, promoting prostitution, and extortion... Marty Chu, has been arrested four times and Tony five, but zero convictions. I can't tell here but from what I was able to find I don't think either of them were ever even indicted for any of their arrests…"

"Nothing huh? Gotta wonder if that's luck, a lazy ADA, poor police work, or if they have the connections to make these things go away? They certainly have the money to make things go away."

As Tommy and Doreen talked about the Chu's, Tommy's phone went off. It was Lisa Yan, Tommy excused himself from the conversation and stepped out of the Squad Room, past Charice and to the top of the stairwell where he could speak privately.

"Hello, Lisa."

"Tommy, I have to tell you something…"

"What's that?"

"I have been placed as the lead investigator of a new task force charged with dismantling the Woo's organization. I can't believe it; my supervisors are even going to let me choose who will be on the team! Oh my God, I am so excited – and I saw the write up in the paper today, good for you, it couldn't have come at a better time. I'm pretty sure it helped, persuade their decision, you know how bosses are when it comes to a press case."

"Do I ever."

"So, we're going to have to get together soon. I'd like your case files from the Li Jun homicide, and I'll get with the ADA too. Bradly, right? Mike Bradly? He's the one assigned, yes?"

"Yes, he is, seems like a decent guy, but be careful who you trust over there. I think there is a leak in that office, how else would anyone know where our witness was lodged? It was Bradly who arranged it all. I really don't think he had anything to do with it, but I do believe somehow the location went from that office to the Chu twins."

"Yeah, thanks for the heads up. I'll be careful who I share any info with and have a serious discussion with whichever ADA is assigned."

"Hey, speaking of the Chu twins, I need to go scoop them up, we just came across two prior known addresses, you wouldn't happen to know where I could find these two, do you?"

"Don't trust anything you see. Those two bounce around like crazy, different apartments all over the city, the both of them are very elusive. Nothing is in their names, whatever you have I'm sure is some phony address they used the last time they got locked up. They do have a pool hall in Queens they frequent almost daily, as well as a club house they use for all their young members and prospects, but you know what? Give me a minute, Hua has a CI in Flushing, if anyone can tell us where the Chu twins are sleeping these days, he'll be able to. I'll ring you back as soon as I hear from him."

"That would be fantastic, Lisa, thank you so much."

"Don't mention it, are you kidding, after all you've done, it's the least I can do. Let me make some phone calls and I'll get back to you as soon as I can."

"Absolutely, and thanks!"

Tommy and Doreen headed out onto the streets. Doreen needed to conduct an interview for one of her cases where there was an ongoing theft problem at a women's clothing store on 86th Street.

About two hours had passed when Tommy got the call he had been waiting on from Lisa, "Hey, Lisa, how you doing?"

"Doing great, Hua's CI came through, you got a pen?"

"Yeah, give me a second… Okay, go ahead."

"Okay, the Chu's have been staying in the second story apartment of 138-22 35th Avenue in Flushing. From what I understand it's a two family, one apartment on street level and another on the second story. He says there is usually a young gang member, or two, outside on a milk crate or sitting on a car as security. If you see any young men in the neighborhood with purple beads, a purple bandana, or a purple dragon tattooed on their chest, know they are Purple Dragons, or at least affiliated, a headless purple dragon tattoo makes them a prospect. The grown-up gang members however wear nothing purple, that identifier is just for the young ones."

"This is great, Lisa, thank you. I'll give you call when we snatch these two up, you can come watch my interviews, and then interview them yourselves for your new task force."

"Hell yeah! and get this – It's been dubbed Operation Dragon Killer."

"Ha, right on, I love it. Alright well, thanks again, and I'm gonna go do some dragon hunting myself. I'll get back to you as soon as anything new comes in."

"Alright, Tommy, have a good night."

"You too."

Tommy turned to Doreen, who sat next to him in the car, "We got ourselves an address, Doreen, and we gonna go catch ourselves some Purple Dragons!"

"Alright there, Saint Michael, when do you think?"

"Well, let's get back to the station house, and see who's available. I'd love to do this first thing tomorrow morning if we can."

"Sounds like a plan, mister man!"

***

After a very brief conversation with Mark Stein, Jimmy Colletti, Sergeant Browne, and Lieutenant Bricks, it was decided that they would attempt to apprehend the Chu twins the following morning at 9:00 AM, at what they believed to be their current residence on 35th Avenue in Flushing.

***

9:14 AM

Tommy and Doreen pulled up just past their destination of 138-22 35th Avenue in Flushing Queens and parked in front of the New Town 99 Cent Discount Store.

It was a simple two-story home, attached to several others, all with a rather sad run-down appearance. Red brick on the first level and a false half-timbered second floor, typical of the area. The house was painted a faded creamy yellow with peeling white trim, the doors to both levels were on the street and both had rusted, grey painted iron gates. Written in black marker on each was the address and 'Downstairs Apt – Upstairs Apt' written on each door.

Tommy and Doreen exited their vehicle and saw Jimmy and Mark pull up two houses down the block and waited for them to exit their vehicle. Both pairs of detectives approached the building from either side.

"This is the place, let's ring the bell and see who answers." said Tommy.

He rang the bell and they waited for a minute. A young Chinese man between sixteen and twenty, wearing purple and black beads around his neck foolishly opened both the interior door and then the rusty grey iron gate, he spoke clearly, but with a heavy accent.

"Yeah, who are you?"

"Hey, how you doing? We're from housing and urban development, would you be Marty or Tony Chu?" Tommy asked as kindly as he could.

"Nah," the young man said with a smile, "They upstairs, you want I…" Tommy interrupted the young man by grabbing him by the throat and yanking him swiftly from the doorway and quickly spinning him around and forcing him to his knees a couple of feet to the left of the doorway. The youth's purple bandana became visible neatly folded and hanging eight inches or so out of his back pocket, "No, that's okay son, we're going to have you sit right here for a minute and I'm going to go upstairs and introduce myself to the both of them –how many others are up there?"

"Fuck you cop." The young man answered.

Crack! Was the sound of Tommy's hand harshly slapping the back of the young man's head, as he tightened the cuffs around his wrists and pulled them up higher to a very uncomfortable position.

"How many are up there!" Tommy demanded, in a low very stern voice, right next to the young man's ear.

"Four, there's four, Marty and Tony and two girls." The young man said, the pain of Tommy's arm bending revealing itself in the young man's voice.

"Jimmy, come with me. Doreen, Mark, stay here with this kid, and keep an eye up at the windows, just in case."

All three acknowledged Tommy with their eyes. Tommy led the way with Jimmy a few steps behind. It was a narrow staircase with a wood banister to the right, as luck would have it, the steps were covered in an old, filthy tan carpeting that muffled their footsteps. The detectives pulled their weapons from their holsters and slowly made their way up the stairs.

Just as Tommy got to the top of the staircase and the arched entry way that led right to the living area, or left to the kitchen, one of the musclebound twins stepped out of the kitchen. It was Marty Chu, startled by the sight of Tommy, he immediately stepped forward and threw a kick with his left foot which hit Tommy hard right in the sternum, sending him back about four feet into the wall behind him.

Tommy barely had a chance to raise his weapon or finish shouting, "Police don't move!" when a second kick came flying his way, Tommy took the hard sharp blow to his ribs on his left side. He trapped Marty's leg under his arm, then he quickly stepped forward, stealing Marty's balance and spun to his right while simultaneously striking Marty in the side of his head with his .9mm Smith and Wesson 5946 duty weapon.

The combination of Tommy's footwork and hard shot to Marty's head sent Marty Chu flying down the stairs. Jimmy, who was still about four steps below the second floor, ducked so quickly and deeply that he was almost in the prone position on the steps as Marty flew right over him, just barely skimming Jimmy's back along the way.

Marty let out a loud shriek as he bounced off the two bottom steps and received a compound fracture to his left shin bone upon making his final landing in the entranceway of the home. Doreen stood just a few feet away with her pistol drawn and commented, "Ouch! I bet that hurts, doesn't it?" In her usual sarcastic style, "Now quit your cryin' bitch and keep your fuckin' hands where I can see em! Mark," she shouted over her shoulder "We're gonna need a bus for this one, his leg is bent into a J shape, and there's a lot of blood!"

Stein nodded his head, his eyes continued to dart from the second story windows to the doorway where Doreen, Marty, and the yet unidentified younger gang member were.

Tommy immediately turned to again face the entry way, as he did, he saw Tony Chu rushing toward him, with a short bat in his hand. As Tommy raised his pistol Tony grabbed Tommy's wrist with his left hand and swung the bat with his right, Tommy reacted quickly blocking the blow of the bat with his left forearm then stepped in close landed a sharp headbutt to Tony's nose and they both fell to the floor, Tony holding tight to Tommy's pistol wrist, and Tommy holding on tight to Tony's bat wielding wrist, they both struggled violently to gain control.

All struggling immediately ceased when Jimmy gave Tony a hard kick to the ribs and then stuck his pistol in his eye shouting "It's over!"

Tony released his grip and put his hand on his head then Tommy spun him onto his stomach and cuffed him then barked at Tony, "Who else is here?" as his eyes scanned the room for anyone else who may be present.

As Tommy stepped toward the front of the room, he could hear someone in the bedroom, "Police! Come out now, with your hands up!"

Slowly, two young Chinese women, in their early twenties, made their way out of the bedroom. They were both dressed fashionably in tight skinny jeans, high boots, oversized sweaters, and overdone makeup. It was obvious these women were more likely girlfriends than prostitutes.

They looked afraid, and one of them shook slightly, as Tommy continued to bark at them, "Who else is in there?"

"No one." One of the two answered.

"Who else is in there?" Tommy yelled even louder.

"No one! No one, I swear, just us!" the girl repeated loudly and frantically.

"Okay then, both of you, turn around and slowly get on your knees, cross your legs at the ankle, now, put your hands behind your head." Both women listened to each command.

"You good, Jimmy?"

"Yeah, good here."

"You good down there, Doreen? Mark?" Tommy yelled loudly.

"We're good, Tommy, our boy is gonna need a bus!" Doreen's shout could be heard faintly coming up the stairs from the sidewalk below.

"Okay, well it looks like we got what we came for. Here take these, Jim," Tommy said as he handed a pair of cuffs to Jimmy, "Cuff one of these two, please." Then he reached behind his waist, pulled out a second pair of handcuffs and handed them to Jimmy, as he finished with the first young woman.

"Keep an eye on these three, I'm gonna clear these rooms."

Tommy slowly and methodically made his way through each room, touching nothing just looking for any additional people who may be in the apartment. He found none.

***

It took some time, but after the arrest of Marty, Tony, and the younger man, Jimmy Ping, the detectives received a warrant to search the premises. In doing so, they recovered a bag containing eighty grams of fentanyl, worth twelve to sixteen thousand dollars, two Ruger EC9 pistols, one Winchester 1300 shotgun, several knives, machetes, swords, and other weapons as well, and boxes of different caliber ammunition amounting to thousands of rounds, as well as just over eighty-six thousand dollars in cash stowed away in two separate shoe boxes.

Marty Chu was taken to New York Presbyterian Hospital and Tony Chu, Jimmy Ping, and the two young women were all transported back to the 2-1. Tony was booked for the attempted abduction of Min. The young man, Jimmy Ping, was interviewed by Tommy, and then again by Lisa, who took his pedigree (personal information, height weight etc.) and photos of him, but neither got anything worthwhile from him. They both interviewed the two women, who also had nothing to add to their investigations, and all three were then released.

Marty was booked, and eventually arraigned bedside, as his injuries kept him in the hospital, cuffed to his bed with a 24-hour police officer stationed outside his room for just over two weeks, as the doctors had to perform two surgeries to pin his leg back together.

All of this kept the squad working throughout the day and well into the next tour. Although no useful information came from any of their interviews, a serious blow was dealt to the Woos and the Purple Dragon organization. Two of their most dangerous lieutenants were now off the streets for the near foreseeable future, at least.

Li Jun

Chapter Nineteen

Tommy woke up to his phone's alarm. American Pinup playing Strongbow was still the song he had queued up, as it played, JoJo began dancing all over the bed with excitement to get his day started. Tommy did his morning fifty, took JoJo out for a walk, showered, and dressed, and headed out the door after kissing his mother goodbye.

It was chilly out, but he decided to walk. He enjoyed his walks to the precinct when he stayed at his mother's place. On the way, he stopped at H&H bagels on 2nd Avenue for two dozen assorted bagels with some cream cheese and butter on the side. After Doreen, Keogh, and Volpe had all mentioned Tommy's bagel deliveries two days before, he felt a large batch to say thanks for the help would somehow be appropriate, and maybe even get a laugh.

About three blocks from the precinct, his phone went off. It was Lisa,

"Hey, Lisa, how you doin'?"

"Good morning, my friend! I have never been better, Tommy. I received another flash drive from your informant, and I haven't slept a wink! This new drive uncovered evidence of the Woos ordering a hit on a missing businessman, a man we've been searching for, for almost eighteen months, and another for two missing Thai drug dealers from Queens. You know who they placed that murder for hire with?"

"I'm pretty sure I know, but I won't steal your thunder, I know you want to say it out loud, don't you?"

"Yes, I do! It was Marty and Tony, fucking Chu! – We got them Tommy! We got all four of them conspiring to murder three different men, all who have gone missing over the last year and a half. Oh my God! I haven't slept in days, but I have never been more energized in my life!"

"This is fantastic news! Good for you, and good work, no, excellent work! You took it and you ran with it!"

"No wait, that's not it, I have Teddy Lo, numerous, numerous messages between Teddy Lo and Peter Woo, talking about the brothels, reporting on sums of money, talking about several different locations, punishing girls, which girls are sick and need a doctor, the doctors name that they use, but wait, wait, you just wait! – are you ready?

Tommy laughed, "Yes, I'm ready."

"I have two names, two very special names for you."

"C'mon with the drama now! Just spill it, the anticipation is…"

"Kai!"

Tommy stopped dead in his tracks, "What?" He couldn't believe what he just heard Lisa say.

"Kai, Agent Kai! Her name comes up several times in different threads."

"And you're sure it's our Kai?"

"Well, the only way it's not her, is if there's more than one Kai, in the FBI, that's working here in New York, so yeah, it's definitely our Kai."

"Holy shit - did this take a turn… You said two names, is the other one from the DA's office?"

"Hang on -- are you ready?"

"For Christ's sake, Lisa, stop foolin' around."

"Swalstein!"

"Swalstein?... Wait a minute, I know that name?"

"Yes! Ethan Swalstein, the U.S Congressman from Queens, his name also comes up repeatedly, and in more than one thread."

"Holy shit! This is gonna be a bombshell!"

"More like a nuclear warhead! We have only started unraveling these emails and text messages, and already we have enough information to lock up at least eight of the Woo organization's associates. We have a special ADA assigned to anything our new task force puts together. Tomorrow, we hope to serve warrants on six different brothels, four different apartments, two restaurants, and a pool hall. The idea is to hit them all simultaneously, fast and hard, before the word gets out that we're onto them."

"Excellent. Wow, you put this all together in just three days?"

"Well, so much of this we were already working on, but these flash drives gave us the hard corroborating evidence we needed to put it all in one package for the DA's office. Like I said, my supervisors are very eager to stay ahead of this. They like our unit, and know this is their time to shine, or take a beating once it all goes public and people think they didn't act, so yeah, the push is on!"

"And no fears on their end about the political fallout, between Kai and Swalstein? You know that's gonna be big news when it hits."

"No, in fact when we spoke about it last night, I think it solidified their resolve to take these cases as far as we possibly can. You know all we do, Tom, is lock 'em up. What I'm curious to see is how the DA's office is going to handle the news. With what we have on Kai and Swalstein now, it's unclear if we'll be arresting them now. Kai has been in direct contact with Peter Woo, but we don't have her committing any crimes yet... She does, in one message tell him: 'Be careful next week.' But we have no clue what it's in regard to."

"Fuck me, Kai is in with them. I didn't care for her from the get-go, but I just assumed she was a cutthroat looking to capitalize off of other people's work. I never imagined she was in the Woo's pocket. And what about this Swalstein cunt?"

"We have him on a back and forth with Mama Woo, talking about a youth benefit in their district, and how much money they are going to raise, as well as two other fund-raising conversations. We have a date where it looks like Swalstein and his assistant, were going to have dinner with both Woos at the Guan Fu restaurant. No crimes yet, but this is certainly going to look bad for him once we finish up with this operation... I am so very curious to see what we get tomorrow, and where it all goes in the end."

"Man, oh man, you really jumped into it, didn't you? Good luck, Lisa, kick ass, take names, and please be careful with yourself, and with the investigation as a whole… You're gonna rock it this week, I know it!"

"Oh, thank you so much, Tommy, thank you for everything. I'll call you later today or tomorrow. In a few days, after most of the smoke has cleared from tomorrow, I'd like to buy you dinner to celebrate and say thanks, please."

"Absolutely, kid, this time you name the place, good luck and stay safe."

"Yes, I will, bye bye."

Tommy grinned from ear to ear the rest of the way to the precinct and up the stairs to the squad room. The place was quiet, the only person in at the time was Stein, who, true to form, was reading the newspaper at his desk.

"Morning, Mark. Got some bagels here, you like me to fix you one?"

"Morning, Tom, no not just yet. I'll come pick one out in a bit, I'm reading about this Chinese shit again in today's paper. That Nunez kid can write."

"Again?" Tommy asked, as if he were surprised, "Seemed like he covered it pretty well the other day, what's he talking about now?"

"Looks like he's digging a little deeper, talking about the Woos again, mentions the human trafficking, but this time he really hammers them and Chinese organized crime in general as the world's preeminent manufacturers and distributors of fentanyl, takes up a whole page, and finishes it up with:

"As the federal government turns its back to the war on drugs, cities like ours find itself indebted to our own police departments, who employ hero cops like Detective Thomas Keane of the 21st precinct, who along with his squad took down Tony and Marty Chu yesterday in Flushing, Queens. The two twin brothers are the leaders of the notorious Purple Dragons gang and were busted in a raid where large amounts of fentanyl, numerous firearms, and thousands of rounds of ammunition were seized."

Tommy stayed silent as he buttered up an onion bagel, then sat at Doreen's desk, opened his bottle of orange juice, and finally said, "Alright, hand it over & let me get a look at that."

He read the article; it was a well written, damning piece of press, it again named the Woos, and the Chus, and he knew it would do what its intent was, to get the attention of the DA's office, and Mayor's office, and no doubt get some phones ringing all over the city.

Tommy kept his cool but was smiling inside, "It is well written, isn't it? I wish this fucker would stop using my name, though."

"C'mon, it's good for you, Tom, maybe you'll finally make grade with all this attention coming your way? You've been a hot commodity lately, especially after that Hayden Marshall case."

"I doubt it, Mark…" came from the entrance of the squad room.

Sergeant Browne interjected as he stepped through the doorway,

"They'll never promote him. Tommy can run circles around most investigators, but we all know he does tend to step on his dick on occasion, don't ya, Tom? And those empty suits at One Police Plaza? They don't like any cowboy shit and our man Keane here hasn't been able to figure out how to keep his horse in the stable or hang his six guns on the wall just yet. Nope. He's still too cowboy, too unorthodox for 'em to make grade."

Tommy furrowed his brow; he wasn't quite sure if Sergeant Browne was looking to start some shit and if he was supposed to be insulted by his comments.

But Browne continued, now speaking directly to Tommy instead of Mark. "And thank God for that, because if you were playing by their rules, Tom, if you were politically motivated at all, if you cared about anything more than getting the bad guys, well sir, you'd be half the detective you are, and then I wouldn't admire you as much as I do."

Mark began to lightly clap his hands, as he did Doreen entered the Squad Room with Lieutenant Bricks right behind her.

"What's going on, what you clapping about, Mark?" Doreen asked.

"You two missed it - it was beautiful. Sergeant Browne here, just came out of the closet and asked Keane for a date."

"Really? I did always think you were keeping something from us, Sarge. So, Tommy? Did you accept his proposal?"

"Why, yes I did, we'll be supping at the Russian Tea Room, then taking in a show this weekend, not that it's any of your business, young lady."

***

For the most part, the rest of the squad's day was mundane. Tommy and Doreen headed out to a couple of calls and did a couple of interviews, while Mark and Jimmy did the same.

Tommy and Doreen took a ride downtown and checked on Min, who appeared to have gained a little bit of weight and was looking much healthier. When she was told about the arrests of the Chu Twins, she laughed and cried simultaneously. It hit her hard emotionally, but in a good way, as if an enormous weight had been lifted from her chest.

The detectives explained how it would still be a process, and how she would remain in the care of the city for some time, before being free to do whatever she wanted. She may be placed in a witness protection program, but for the moment, they assured her that she was safe in their care.

As they drove back to the precinct, Tommy's phone went off. It was Lisa Yan again, "Hey, Lisa, what's up?"

"Got some bad news for you."

"Really, what's that?"

"We have word that the Woos are on the lam. We believe they are in Toronto."

"Ahh fuck me! And fuck that fucking judge for giving Mama Woo such a low bail, fuck, she shouldn't have gotten any bail at all… Fuck!" he exclaimed, while pounding his hand on the steering wheel in frustration and disbelief.

"We alerted the Toronto PD and Interpol, but really, we know nothing, nothing more than they're in Toronto."

"Well, fuck me! There's nothing we can do about it now, hopefully they can grab them up there, and hopefully extradite them back here to us."

"Sorry, Tom, wanted to let you know right away. Have a good evening."

"You too, dear, and hey - good luck tomorrow, like I said, I know you're gonna rock it."

"Thanks, I'll call you tomorrow when it's all over, and hey to you -- another great article in the paper again today, good for you!"

Tommy hung up, "Woos escaped to Toronto I take it?" Doreen asked glumly.

"Yup, fuckers are in the wind."

"You think they'll get scooped up?"

"I doubt it, Doreen, they got more money than God, and more connections than we can imagine. Shit, they're in the wind, probably be in Hong Kong, Taiwan, fuckin Switzerland, Panama... Who knows where they'll be before we even sign out from tour today. Fuck me. I really wanted them to go away and pay for that little girl's life. All the awful shit they've done, all the pain they're responsible for, I so wanted to put them away, for Li, that poor little child. Fuck me!"

Tommy went silent after that. Doreen felt it too, but could see it hit Tommy particularly hard, she put her hand on

Tommy's forearm as he held the steering wheel, with that quiet recognition that only cops do.

They parked the car and as they made their way up the sidewalk towards the precinct, Doreen stopped and said, "It's only another thirty minutes till end of tour Tommy, just go on home, I'll sign you out."

Tommy stoic as always replied, "No, I can go sign myself out." With a little indignation in his voice.

Doreen stepped closer and put her arms around him, as she hugged him, she said softly in his ear, "Go home, Tommy, I'll sign you out."

"Thank you." He replied, also softly, giving into what Doreen was trying to do for him.

He turned and started walking east toward First Avenue. Doreen stood and watched him until he was out of sight.

On his walk back to his mother's place, he made his way over to 80th Street, and over to 439. He stood in front of the building, just as he had the week before. He took a deep breath, and stepped up to the wrought iron fence, he gripped it with both hands firmly and looked up to the window where Li had been thrown to her death, "I'm sorry, Li. I'm so sorry, I made a promise, and I failed you," His eyes moved to the frieze of Minerva, he had no more words as he stared into her stone eyes.

Doreen was right. The death of Li did hit him hard, maybe harder than he ever thought it would. His hands loosened their grip and dropped to his sides, and he headed home to his mother's feeling completely hollow.

Once home, he let himself in, tumbling the locks on his mother's door, he could hear little JoJo's feet dancing on the hardwood floors behind the door, "Hiya, Ma, I'm home. Does JoJo need a walk?"

"Hiya, Tommy, no, Tommy, no, I just had him out, you have a good day today, Tommy?"

"Yes, ma'am, I had a fine day, thanks, I'm a little tired though, I'm gonna go lie down for a bit, I think."

"Okay, Tommy dear, get some rest, you'll feel better after you do, Tommy."

He went into his room, closed the door, and sat on the edge of the bed. As he did, JoJo began scratching at the door, Tommy got up and opened the door and gently pushed JoJo away with his foot, "Not now, boy, go see grandma." He reentered and sat back down, only to hear JoJo scratching again for entry. Tommy again went to the door and opened it, the little dog sat there looking up at Tommy with a perplexed look on his face. "You're not gonna stop, are you? Okay, come on in."

Tommy sat on the edge of the bed and JoJo sat on the floor watching him. Tommy then stood and removed his coat, he took his .9-millimeter pistol out of its holster and placed it on the side table, then his .38 revolver, and his handcuffs.

He sat back down, and a tear ran down his cheek, his elbows rested on his knees and his head in his hands, as another, then another tear appeared. He had seen so much pain and suffering in his life, and this certainly wasn't the first time a case had gotten to him, but for some reason the Woos skipping the country hit him hard. He genuinely felt that he had failed Li. Of course, he hadn't, he had done all he could, in fact he had done more than most probably would, but now knowing the Woos were gone, he was at a loss, and his frustration overwhelmed him.

His tears stopped, he wiped his eyes, then again softly murmured to himself, "Fuck me, I am so sorry, Li." Tommy then lay back in his bed, and little JoJo hopped up from the floor and joined him. Slowly and cautiously JoJo approached, knowing something was wrong, he placed his right paw on Tommy's chest, and they both sat quietly for a minute. Tommy stroked the dog a few times and JoJo feeling comforted, curled up tight next to Tommy, and sighed.

A few more minutes passed, and Tommy picked up his phone. He texted his daughter, Caitlin "OXXO, Love you, Girl." Was all he wrote, then a message to his ex-wife Cookie "OXXO." And after a moment of contemplation, Gil Nunez, "Tomorrow, midday?"

Chapter Twenty

The following morning came quick, he checked his phone, it was forty minutes before his alarm was to go off. There were a few texts he had slept through, the night before.

His daughter, Caitlin, "I love you too Daddy, school is fine, miss you!!!

His ex-wife, Cookie, "xo, all okay with you?" was her response.

Gil Nunez, "Absolutely, what time?"

Roya. "Get with me first thing in the morning, I have something for you before you leave for work."

JoJo crawled out from under the covers and licked Tommy's cheek, before he rolled onto the floor for his morning fifty. He then messaged Roya back, "Sorry I missed your message, I was sleeping, you available in twenty?"

Tommy then took JoJo out, and while walking, messaged Gil, "How about noon, the Globe again?"

After he came back home, he showered, shaved, and was dressing when he received a reply from Roya, "Sure, message me when you're leaving."

"In another ten." Was Tommy's answer.

And in a few minutes, he kissed his mother on the head and stepped out to the hallway, then out onto the stoop, he looked left, then right, scanning the block, then leaned against the handrail and waited a moment for Roya to appear.

"Morning, Tommy, how are you?"

"Doing alright, kid, how are you?"

"Great thanks, come on, let's walk down to 86th and I'll catch the train. Here, here is another flash drive for your linguist. How is the investigation going? I am picking up a lot of chatter and it seems like these people are in a bit of a shambles from the little I can make out. I also saw this case has been in the paper and, yesterday a reporter doing an expose on the Woos was interviewed on television, you're definitely making some waves!"

"No, it's not me, it's the information you're digging up that's making waves, and a very enthusiastic detective from the Asian Gang Unit. You two are going to right a lot of wrongs in the next few months I think."

Roya smiled; she loved hearing that.

As they made their way to Lexington Avenue they discussed the case, and how vile the Woos and the Purple Dragons were. Tommy again explained how dangerous the situation was and how Roya needed to be careful, cool, and never let anyone know what she had been able to do.

Roya realized how much she loved Tommy talking to her as if she were his daughter. She knew there was nothing disrespectful about the way he spoke to her, as if she were still a child. In fact, she took it as a verbal embrace. One of deep respect and love. He cared enough to reiterate the point to be cautious, and he had entrusted her with so much responsibility.

At the 86th Street subway station, they stopped, and had a little hug, then went their separate ways.

Tommy arrived at the precinct about ten minutes early. He sat alone and began going over a few cases he had let fall behind. Slowly each of the other members of the squad filed in. Charice made her way in, loud, boisterous, and cheerful as always, she broke the silence of the room with.

"Quiet night in the ol' 2-1, last night. Here's a domestic for you, Detective Doyle. An aggravated harassment, and a vandalism, known perp for you, Detective Stein. Two cars broken into on East End and First Avenues for you, Detective Colletti, and for our handsome celebrity over here, Detective Keane, we have another domestic dispute, this one with injury."

As Charice finished, Mark mentioned, "The paper skipped you today, handsome, Detective Keane... Nunez is talking about Chinese organized crime again but left you out of it today."

"Wow, again?" Doreen chimed in, "The killing of that little prostitute really opened a can of ass kickin' up for that gang, didn't it?"

"What are they talking about today?" Jimmy asked.

"Today it's all about their international connections and how the Woos, and other groups of snakeheads, bring thousands of people a year here to the U.S. and other western countries. How some are sold into slavery, how others sell themselves, and how many are duped into a life of virtual slavery believing they left China for good paying jobs - only to find they are paid nothing and worked to death."

"Hand it over when you're done, please?" Tommy asked.

"Here, read it, it's good." Mark handed him the paper. It was another damning piece; Tommy was curious what would come after his meeting with Gil in the next few hours.

***

12:03 PM

Tommy arrived at The Globe. The same bartender was washing glasses behind the bar, that had been there the previous week. He sat at the same table where he and Gil had sat the last time they met there. The pub was still quiet, having just opened, and only two men sat at the bar, one with his nose in the paper, the other staring up at the television.

A few minutes later Gil arrived, "Detective Keane, how are you today?"

"Tommy, please Gil, call me Tommy."

"Of course, I'm sorry, how are you, Tommy?"

"I'm doing well and how you doing today?"

"Great! Have you been keeping up with the expose I've been doing? We are getting a lot of attention; I even had a TV interview last night. So, yeah, I'm doing great, and thank you again for turning me onto this story, I hope you are getting the pressure you wanted out of it."

"Gil, I couldn't be much happier. My hope was for people to take this story seriously, and hopefully, maybe take one or two of these savages down. It looks like that may be the case. Sadly, I heard, and wanted you to know, that both Mama and Peter Woo have fled the country."

"No," shaking his head in disbelief, "Well that's some shit news, do you have any idea where they went?"

"From what I understand they are in Toronto."

"Oh man, that sucks, do you think the local PD will pick them up for you?"

"I am certain they would, but personally I'm gonna guess they are in the wind. They have the money and the connections. I would bet they're long gone from Canada already, but who knows?"

"Well, thanks for that bit of info, I'll definitely touch on that for the next piece, and come down hard on that judge that let them post bail, anything else you think you can share?"

"Yes, something pretty serious."

"What's that?"

"There is an FBI Agent and a sitting U.S. Congressman mixed up in this somehow, I'm not sure how or..."

Gil softly interrupted. "Ethan Swalstein?"

"So, you know something about him?"

"I have been digging deep into these people now for the last week, ever since we first spoke. I have seen Swalstein turn up again and again, nothing more than he just keeps popping up. I have a photo of him in a restaurant with Peter Woo, and another with him at a ribbon cutting ceremony for some youth program in Queens. Standing just behind him is Mama Woo. Also, and this may mean nothing, but I have seen numerous photographs now with him at events; at community dinners, parades, you name it, and he always seems to be accompanied by a nice looking, young, Asian woman. I mean, that's nothing on the face of it right, but, well, have you seen this guy? He is no looker, yet time and time again he has some young, hot, Asian girl on his arm. Just seems off to me?"

"Yeah, well that's why I'm mentioning it. These Woos have been terrorizing their own people. All over the city for at least a decade, doing murders, selling drugs, and running prostitutes. Every time one of their members is collared, the case is dropped before it hits the grand jury. So yeah, I'm thinkin', no I'm sayin', they are politically hung. And they have enough juice to make cases just vanish, so whoever is in their pocket, must be big. Then, there also seems to be an FBI connection... this I don't know much about, and I won't mention any names yet, but I think you should keep an eye out in that direction. You know... Be aware of it, because again, there is a suspicious connection of some kind going on there too."

"Yeah, this thing is quite a tangled mess, and nothing would surprise me at this point. Anything else I may be interested in Tommy? Not that this isn't a lot to run with at the moment."

"There is a woman, a female detective, her name is Yan, she works in the Asian Gang Unit, and she's on the level. I think you may like to get with her. She is going to have her hands full today, but going forward... If this story still has legs for you, she is the one to build a relationship with, like I said, she's on the level and you can trust her."

"Awesome, thanks for the heads up, can I, should I mention your name?

"Yes, like I said you can trust her, she's good people, just be cool."

"Always."

***

Tommy and Gil had just one drink and skipped lunch. Then each returned to their own worlds, and workloads. At about 3:15 in the afternoon, Tommy was back at the 2-1 when his phone went off, with a call from Lisa, "Hey Lisa how you doing?

"Oh my God, great, Tommy, do you have a minute for me?"

"Absolutely, let me step out into the hallway where I can hear you better. There, go ahead, tell me how it went today?"

"Yeah, that's why I called; I've been dying to tell you. All went perfectly as planned, all thirteen warrants went off without a single problem. We locked up a total of twenty-eight suspected gang members, including Teddy Lo, and took thirty-two sex workers into custody, seventeen firearms, and ton of assorted edged weapons. We're still counting the money, and the drugs, but the money is going to be in the tens of thousands, and the drugs will certainly be in the kilos. And we also got books, several books that they were keeping records with, loaded with names and addresses. This case is going to be undisputable, Tommy, oh God, I am so happy with today!"

"Alright! This is what I like to hear, listen, if a young reporter named Gil Nunez comes calling..."

"He's the one who has been doing the write ups on the Woos, yes, I have been following him."

"That's the guy, if he comes calling, know he is a decent guy, tell him what you want. Remember, he is a reporter but he's a good guy, he's honest and he won't try to hurt you, something tells me after today, you may be hearing from him."

"Okay. I gotta go, Tommy, they're calling me. I just wanted to thank you one more time, for all you've done to help make today happen."

"It's nothing, Lisa, you did all the work, go on now, kick ass..."

"And take names! Bye bye!"

Tommy stuffed his phone into his pocket and went back into the Squad Room where he told the others about the call he got from Lisa Yan and how she and her team had just locked up twenty-eight of the Purple Dragons and other Woo associates, including Teddy Lo.

Chapter Twenty-One

5:10 PM

Tommy's phone went off, he saw it was Roya and picked up immediately.

"Hey, Roya, how you doing, kid?"

"Not so good at the moment," she replied with a rather panicked voice, "They're going to try to kill you, Tommy... The Purple Dragons have put a hit out on you. I intercepted an email from Teddy Lo to Peter Woo, basically saying they won't have to worry about you much longer, and that some headless dragons, whatever they are, will be taking care of you very soon. And that The Woos will be able to return from Canada once you are gone."

"Really." Tommy answered, sounding rather unimpressed.

"That's all you have to say? 'Really?' These people are talking about killing you, Tommy." Roya raised her voice.

"Yeah, that's what it sounds like... Don't get me wrong, Roya, I don't like the sound of that. I'm not looking to leave this planet anytime soon. And I'm going to take it very seriously, but there's not a lot I can do about it. If they come for me, I'm just going to have to be ready for them, and watch my back."

"Watch your back? What do you mean watch your back? You don't have eyes in the back of your head, Tommy, these Purple Dragons are no joke! I've been reading up on them and they are a brutal, brutal, bunch."

"Yeah, I know, I'll be careful, trust me. This certainly isn't the first time some perps, or gangsters, have threatened to take me out. It's one of those things that uh, you know… Comes with the territory."

"I don't like that your being so fucking flippant about this. I'm telling you, they say they are going to kill you, so the Woos can come back to New York. These people are afraid of you, Tommy, and they want to get rid of you."

"I know, Roya, I believe you, and believe me I'm going to take it seriously, you know what? I won't go back to 88th Street until this shit blows over. I'll stay at my place in White Plains, so no one follows me home to 88th, and that will keep my Ma, you, your Ma, and anyone else safe. I really doubt anyone knows where I live or is going to head all the way up there to kill me, and like I just said, these fuckers, these gangbangers, are always talking shit about killing cops, but it's a rare, rare, thing when they follow through with it. Believe me, I've had very credible threats made on my life by some very scary people over the years. Don't sweat it kid, alright? I'm always careful."

"I don't like it … I don't like it."

"I know, I know you don't, and I appreciate your concern. But believe me, these mutts are all about the bravado, killing a cop would bring the full force of the NYPD down on their heads, and Peter and Mama Woo are very shrewd businesspeople. They don't want anything to do with us, or the heat some of the larger Tongs are already breathing down their necks. Killing a cop is the last thing any of them want to have on their plate. But I promise, I promise I will be careful, and I'll avoid going home to Ma's place for the next couple days or even weeks. Hopefully, you'll see the cop killing chatter melt away to nothing, and I'll bet you anything you'll hear that Peter and Mama Woo, are out of power and someone new has taken over all their rackets before you know it."

"Okay, I wish you sounded more concerned, but okay, if you say so... just please stay safe... please."

"I will, I promise... Listen, I got to go, alright? I'm finishing something up then I have a long drive up to White Plains tonight... Thanks for the heads up, Roya, I appreciate it."

"Goodnight, Tommy, be careful."

***

8:32 PM

Tommy parked his CRV, in his normal spot, in the lot on Mitchell Street which was located directly behind his building. As he opened the vehicles door, and stepped out, he took his Smith and Wesson centennial revolver from between his legs and dropped it into the left pocket of his coat. He adjusted his pants from the ride up and then locked the car.

Rather than entering the rear of his building, as he normally would have, Tommy left the parking lot from its entrance on Mitchell Street and made a right heading towards Mamaroneck Avenue. He was a little hungry after the drive and decided to grab a bite before heading up to his apartment for a little TV before bed.

Tommy thought about the weeks' investigation and what had been uncovered. He was quite unhappy at the thought of the hit the Woo's placed on him, but at the same time he was thrilled with the number of arrests that had been made. He thought about the women and children that had been liberated from their lives of sex slavery and the large number of drugs and weapons that were seized. With the help of Gil Nunez, writing story after story about the Purple Dragons, he felt the DA's office would go full steam ahead with prosecutions on all involved in this sordid mess of sex, drugs, and violence.

Even if Tommy would never be able to get any retribution for Li Jun's individual death, he knew, or at least felt, her life would not be lost in vain. Already, at the very least, he, Lisa, and their respective teams had dealt a heavy blow both financially and organizationally to the Woos and the Purple Dragons. If he could maybe dismantle this gang then possibly, just possibly, he may have done the right thing by young Li Jun and her life, and death, as horrid as both were, may not have been for nothing.

Tommy headed to the corner of Mamaroneck and Martine Avenues to the Famous Famiglia Pizzaria.

"Vinny! You handsome bastard, how you doing pal?" Tommy said, as he entered, to the large man with the bright smile behind the counter.

"Tommy! Where you been? We haven't seen you in months... Where the hell you been, man?"

"I've been staying in the city a lot these days. I got transferred from the Bronx a few months ago and it's just easier, so now I'm there more than I'm here, it seems."

"Well, I see they are keeping you busy. I saw you in the papers for that Nun case, oofa, that looked like a bad one... Also read about those kids you found on Thanksgiving, - nuts! Something now about some Chinese gangsters, no doubt they got you working down there, huh."

"Actually, it's not nearly as busy as the Bronx, but a lot of what happens in Manhattan gets the attention of the papers, that's why you hear about it, no one really gives a shit what happens in the Bronx, unfortunately."

"Yeah... I believe that - the Bronx is like the lost borough of the city, ain't it?"

"Something like that, yeah."

"So, what'll you have, Tommy?"

"How bout' a chicken parm on garlic bread... That, and a large Pepsi from the fountain, please."

"No Pepsi – Coke!" Vinny replied with a smile.

"Yeah, whatever." Tommy replied with a laugh.

Li Jun

Tommy and Vinny made small talk for a bit, then Tommy sat in the back of the Pizzeria and ate his sandwich. Again, Tommy couldn't help but contemplate the case. As open and shut as it was meant to be, he felt he would continue to chase a sense of closure... How could he bring the Woos to justice? they skipped town and all that was known was that they were in Toronto, nothing more. The local authorities, and Interpol, were notified but would anything come of it?

Tommy wiped his mouth, finished his soda, and took the red plastic tray to the trash bin, where he cleared it off and dropped it on top of the bin. He stood for a moment behind a young Puerto Rican mother, and her young son, waiting for them to finish paying for their pizza and chatting with the very affable Vinny, before he himself stepped up to the counter again, and shook Vinny's hand,

"Take care, Vinny, it was nice to see you, my friend."

"Hey you too, Tommy! And hey, be careful and stay safe down in that fuckin' city alright, man? And come back soon!"

"I will, Vin, I'll see you again this week, I'm sure. I'm gonna be up here for maybe a week or two again, or for a little while anyway... I'll be back in soon, all the best."

"Take care, Tommy." He heard one more time from Vinny as he stepped out the door and headed across Mamaroneck Avenue and towards his apartment at 240 Martine Avenue. As he crossed the street, he buttoned up his thick leather coat and stuck his hands deep into the pockets to brace against the cold.

He nodded hello to the barber, who stood in the window of his shop, as he approached his building, who nodded back.

Tommy had come to really like his little neighborhood in White Plains over the last ten years he had lived there. It still wasn't home to him, but there was a friendly familiarity that he enjoyed. White Plains was a small city, and he lived right downtown, so everything he wanted was an easy walk for him. There was plenty of shopping and plenty of restaurants to eat at and bars to drink in just blocks from where he lived. Really, he couldn't ask for more.

He liked his little two-bedroom apartment and his building. The dwelling was a large, handsome, Tudor styled pre-war building built of brown brick with stone trim and half-timbered bay windows that popped out all over it. There were nice, well-kept shrubs and trees in the courtyard and entranceway of the building that softened the cityscape a bit. Yes, Tommy liked his building and liked White Plains. He thought maybe he was missing it a bit more now that he was spending most of his time back at his mother's place in the old neighborhood.

Staying in the City was certainly more convenient, and there was something romantic about walking those streets again on a daily basis. But there was no doubt in Tommy's mind that the old neighborhood, Yorkville, was no longer his. It had become too gentrified over the years, and most everything he had loved was now gone. Sure, there were remnants here and there, faces and voices from his past. But now he felt he had a stronger bond with the streets of the Bronx, where he had spent nineteen years working, than the neighborhood he had spent half his life growing up in.

Tommy entered the half circle walkway, that led up to the entrance of his building, when he heard a car door slam loudly behind him. As he turned to see where the noise was coming from, he felt a hard, and pinpointed punch, above his right collar bone along with a loud *pop pop pop*. That punch he felt was a bullet. Tommy spotted two Asian teenagers, who were maybe sixteen years of age in almost identical black track suits, running up the walkway firing pistols at him. Tommy stepped back into an interview stance, (which is similar to a boxer's stance,) and pulled his 38 Smith and Wesson Centennial from his left coat pocket, while he reached for his Smith and Wesson 5946 .9mm that he had holstered on his right hip, and immediately returned fire.

He hit the first young man, who was now only about fifteen feet away from him, in the forehead right above his left eye with his first shot. He then pulled the trigger two more times, hitting the second teenager in his right shoulder and left hip. The second teenager then fell backwards from taking the two bullets Tommy had hit him with, and as he fell, he continued to fire rapidly *pop pop pop pop pop,* from a 9mm Ruger Security 9. One of the bullets hit Tommy in the head, just above his right ear.

Tommy dropped, his body making an audible thud as he hit the pavement. He lay lifeless in front of his building, his right hand still gripping the .9mm that never left its holster.

Travis Myers & Natasha Myers Marsiguerra

Li Jun

Travis Myers & Natasha Myers Marsiguerra

Li Jun

Chapter Twenty-Two

2:58 AM White Plains Hospital.

Tommy's eye's snapped open. He shook his head, trying to focus his eyes from a fog, he was lost for a moment, having no idea where he was. Then it clicked, he was lying in a hospital bed, he felt drugged, a little nauseous, and very confused.

Slowly his eyes focused. His head began to clear, he took a deep breath, and assessed his situation; 'I'm alive, I don't feel any pain,' he clenched his fists, then wiggled his fingers a bit. He wiggled his toes and bent both of his knees slightly, one, then the next. He raised each of his arms slightly, one then the next, everything seemed to be working fine, but everything felt a little heavy and slow, 'That's the drugs,' he thought to himself. Then he took his hands and slowly felt his torso, nothing felt bad to him, he couldn't find any wounds, and again, no pain.

He scanned his bed and found the nurses button and pressed it.

"Detective Keane, you've decided to join us." A bright eyed, young black nurse, with an enchanting smile, said to him as she entered the room.

"Water, please." Tommy asked.

"Absolutely, Detective, I bet your mouth is dry, isn't it? Sometimes those drugs can really dry your mouth out... How are you feeling?" She asked in a gentle caring voice.

She put a cup of water with a straw to Tommy's mouth.

"Thank, you, I feel... Well, I feel... How do I feel? I feel kind of... Kind of foggy, I guess?"

"Are you in any pain, Mr. Keane?"

"No, I don't think so?"

"Uncomfortable?"

"No... No not at all."

"Okay, well that's a good sign. Do you know what has happened to you?"

"I, I, I'm gonna guess I've been shot, right? I was, there was, they were shooting at me, and I guess they must have hit me because I don't remember anything else -- but I don't find, feel, find, can't find, or feel any wounds."

"Wow, you're doing pretty well in the memory department, Mr. Keane, also a good sign. Yes, you were shot. You were in a gun fight, and you were shot in the right side of your neck and in the right side of your head. Luckily for you, the bullet that hit your head didn't enter your skull. In fact, I heard the doctor's say the wound you received from when your head hit the pavement may be worse that the one you received from the bullet hitting you in the head... But I won't go any further, I'll let the doctors explain everything later."

"The kids?"

"I'm not sure what happened, or what the story is really, but I know you killed one of them… How many were there?"

"I only saw two… Two, I think there were two?"

"Well, you're here with us now, Mr. Keane, and we are happy to have you back… A doctor will be here soon. Also, some detectives want to speak to you as well… There are a whole bunch of people just waiting to speak with you… Here is some more water for now, here take a sip."

"Is he awake?" A voice came from the doorway.

"Yes, he is," the nurse answered, followed by "And I'll leave you two alone now." And she exited the room.

Tommy tried to focus on the doorway. All he saw was a tall man in a long coat, but he could tell by his dress and haircut he was a cop.

"Detective? White Plains?"

"Yes, Detective Dennis Shaffer, take your time, Detective. I'll talk to you when you're ready. You have a couple of your people, and a DEA (Detective's Endowment Association) Rep here as well. They all just went for a coffee and a smoke… We'll wait for them. How are you feeling? I know that's an odd question after taking two bullets, but are you alright? Do you think we can talk tonight?"

"Yeah, yeah, I'm feeling pretty good. I feel a little better, I'm coming out of this daze a little."

"Okay, good, glad you're feeling alright. I'll give you some time and we'll wait for the others to join us. We have some questions, you understand."

"Of course."

Detective Schaffer stepped back outside into the hallway. Tommy laid his head back on the pillow, and slowly ran everything he could remember about the attack through his mind.

It took a second for more of the fog to leave him, but within minutes he had a full picture of what happened in those few seconds, as he approached his building.

'A car door slammed, I turned... I felt something hit me, then heard the popping of a pistol, I returned fire, the first assailant went down, there was a second, I think I hit him too?... Did I?'

He lay silently for approximately another twenty minutes when he was rejoined by Detective Schaffer, and three others; Detectives Columbus and Ritter, both were reps from Tommy's union, the DEA, who were there on his behalf and to aid as representation during the questioning he was about to get from Detective Schaffer; Lieutenant Bricks was also there, who had made the ride up as soon as he was notified of the shooting.

Lieutenant Bricks began, "Hey, Tommy, how you doing? We have your DEA reps here, this is Columbus and Ritter, and this is Detective Schaffer from WPPD. He needs to interview you."

Tommy nodded to each.

"I know you've been through this before, Tom, if you're not up to it yet, you know you don't have to say anything or answer any questions just yet. So don't be shy, everyone can wait till you're ready." Bricks continued.

"No, I'm fine, Lu, I'm fine. There's not much to it, and I remember most of it, but go-ahead fellas, ask me what you are here to ask me."

Detective Ritter spoke up, "Hey, Keane, you know my partner and I are here on your behalf. Just like Lieutenant Bricks said here, you don't have to give a statement yet and you don't have to say anything at all. Detective Schaffer here, of course, needs to investigate what happened in front of your building. If you're comfortable answering his questions, well we're fine with that, as long as you think you are up for it and ready to proceed."

"Yeah sure... Go ahead, Schaffer, ask away, there's really not much to it, but go ahead."

"Okay, Detective Keane, well let me reiterate what your Lieutenant and your rep's have just told you, you don't have to talk to me now."

"I understand, please go ahead."

"Okay, can you tell me... do you remember, where you were and what you were doing at approximately 21:10 this evening?"

"Yes... I was on my way home. I had just finished a sandwich at the pizzeria down the block --The Famous Familia Pizzeria. I had a chicken parm on garlic bread, and a Pepsi, and I had a short conversation with the boss there, Vinny."

"Okay, great, can you tell me what happened next?"

"Sure, I can… I was walking home, and… And as I approached the entrance to the building, I heard a car door slam; I wasn't alarmed but I did turn to see where the noise had come from, and when I did, I felt something hit me in the neck… Then heard shots… I saw a young Chinese kid, small kid, looked like a teenager, charging me and firing a weapon, he got off three or four shots. I returned fire and he fell."

Tommy took a breath and then continued.

"Right behind him was a second kid, also Chinese, also appeared to be a teenager. He was also firing at me; I believe I returned fire… I'm pretty sure I did… Then I woke up in this room with a nice young nurse and a tall detective standing in the door… That was my night… How was yours?"

Detective Schaffer smiled, as did the others.

"I was having a quiet night until some NYPD Detective decided to get shot on my shift, but my wife will send him some cookies to say thanks for the overtime… So, Detective Keane, have you ever seen either of these men before?"

"No, never."

"But I understand you are currently conducting an investigation involving Chinese organized crime?"

"Yes, well I was, the death, the death of a young girl."

"And can you tell me, sir, the name of this organization?"

"The name of the gang is The Purple Dragon's."

"Okay, well here is something that may interest you... You killed one of your attackers, he is Asian, and he appears to be a teenager. You caught him with one round in his forehead just above his left eye... We have no information on him yet, but he does have a tattoo on his left chest. It's of a body of a purple dragon, no head, just the body of a dragon, and it is purple."

"A Headless Dragon." Tommy stated.

"This is of some significance?"

"Yes, Headless Dragons are wannabe members, or more like prospects, to the gang. They're marked as gang property with the headless dragon... then once they have earned full membership, they are allowed to add the head to their tattoos."

"I'm guessing killing you would have earned them their heads?"

"I would imagine so."

"Did you have any idea they were coming for you, Detective? Have there been any threats made on your life?"

"No, none." Tommy answered, remembering full well what Roya had told him earlier.

"Well, we have him and recovered the .9mm Ruger he shot you with. We are looking for a late model black Honda Civic. We have an eyewitness that say's your other assailant, who you also shot and knocked to the ground, scrambled back up and made it into the backseat of that Honda which was being driven by a third Asian male. Right now, every department between here and the City, as well as the State

Police are looking for this vehicle. We have identified the plates and they belong to a stolen black Honda from Queens. Right now, that's all we have."

"Not bad, Schaffer, it's only been a few hours, hopefully these savages will be in custody before the sun is up." Said Lieutenant Bricks in response.

"Let's hope so," Schaffer continued, "I'll leave you to rest now, Detective. I'll, of course, have more questions and be following up with you and coordinating with your squad and anyone else in the NYPD I may need to speak with. But, as of now, I think we're good. Please feel better and know our prayers are with you."

"That's it? Well thanks, Schaffer, I appreciate it, hopefully I can be of more help in a day or two."

Lieutenant Bricks then interrupted, "And we'll share our file and everything we – Tommy, has on this case and these murderous bastards with you too, Detective. Anything you need, just ask." And he handed Detective Schaffer his card.

"Thanks, Lieutenant, I appreciate it."

10:01 AM White Plains Hospital

A short, round nurse, with red hair, entered the room.

"Morning, Detective. You appear to be doing well this morning. Listen, our visiting hours are from noon to 6 pm, but in your case we are making an exception, because you have several family members and coworkers who are lining up outside waiting to get in. But before we let them in, I'm just going to check your vitals and ask you how you're feeling, and if you would indeed like any visitors at the moment."

"Yes, ma'am, I'm feeling pretty good overall. I can now feel some discomfort in the back of my head, and here where my neck meets my shoulder, but nothing too bad, just whenever I move. I get a sharp, stabbing feeling every once in a while, in both locations, mainly my neck but really, it's not too bad... and yes, I'm certainly ready to see whoever has come."

"Okay, great, we'll let them come inside in a moment,"

"Thank you, dear."

***

First to enter the room was Lieutenant Bricks and Doreen Doyle.

"Ahh, look at him—layin' there all cute and humble, like a little boy with a boo boo on his head, and he's in his jammies even, he doesn't look half as bad as you said he did, Lu." Doreen said loudly, with her Doreen smirk. She smiled as she joked, but her eyes told a different story. Doreen was visibly disturbed to see Tommy laid up in his hospital bed with his head and neck bandaged up and tubes and monitors running in and out of him.

"So, we're gonna start it like this are we?" Tommy asked, a broad smile on his face, "Just like you to kick a fella when he's down."

"How you feeling, Tommy?" she asked in a much lower and more somber tone.

"Not bad, to be honest, not bad at all. My neck is stiff and achy, my head only hurts when I touch it... worst part is, from what I understand, is that the bullet that went through my neck ruined my jacket."

"Really? That's the worst part? That's what you're stressing?" Doreen replied like an angry mother, then looking over to Lieutenant Bricks, "Guy almost bites it, takin' two bullets while killing one or more of his assailants, and he's worried about his leather jacket?"

"What can I tell you, Doreen, he's a paratrooper, these airborne guys are all wrong in the head ... just be happy he's on our side."

"Yeah, no doubt."

"Any news on this investigation, Lu?" Tommy asked, "Have we found out anything more since last night?"

"No, nothing yet. Rest assured, every cop in the city and your friends over at the FBI are all over this case. Without a doubt, we should be hearing more very soon, we wanted to stop and see you this morning, make sure you are well, and if you had anything else to add from last night. We have a joint meeting at two this afternoon, to re-hash and reorganize this investigation, right now we have people monitoring everything connected with these people. Watching the airports, seaports, here and in Canada, doing everything we can to catch Mama and Peter Woo, and any of the Purple Dragons we can scoop up..."

"Oh, my fucking God!" Lieutenant Bricks was interrupted by the loud and unmistakable voice of Cookie Keane.

"What did they do to you? Oh my God, my God, look at you," she said, still frozen in the doorway. Their daughter, Caitlin, trying to look in over her shoulder. Cookie then rushed to the side of her ex-husband's bed. She placed her left hand on his chest, and leaned in to kiss him, once, twice, then three and four times. "These motherfuckers! Tell me you killed them, tell me you killed these motherfuckers, Tommy—Oh my God, my God, you and this fucking job, when, when? ..."

Caitlin gently took her mother by the shoulders and pulled her back, "Relax, Mommy, relax. Daddy's gonna be fine, he doesn't need you yelling at him now, he needs some quiet."

"Good morning, Cookie." Tommy said, "Give me a kiss, Caitlin – What? Did Mommy drive up to Siena to get you last night?"

"No, Nick drove me down, then we all drove here this morning. He's parking the car now, just dropped us at the door, and we came right up."

"Ahh, I see and..." Tommy was interrupted.

"How hard can they make it in this place for a mother to come see her son?" Maria Keane with her sister, Sophia, walked through the door, "Tommy, oh, Tommy look at you... You actually look pretty good, Tommy, doesn't he Sophie? Doesn't Tommy look good?"

"I seen him look worse." His aunt Sophia answered.

"Ma, what are you doing up here?"

"What do you think, Tommy? If my Tommy is in the hospital, I'm going to come see him. Sophie and I caught the train up this morning, and, Tommy, your sister Kathleen says hello and hopes you get better soon, she wants you to call her, Tommy, as soon as you have a chance."

"Okay Ma, I…"

"Caitlin, look at how beautiful you are. Look, Sophie, look at our Caitlin and how beautiful she is."

"Beautiful." Sophie replied.

"And Caitlin is smart too, she's in medical school you know, our Caitlin is going to be a doctor."

"I'm just in pre-med right now, Grandma."

"Med, pre-med? What's the difference, your brain is as beautiful as your face, Caitlin." Maria said with a big smile, then in a more somber tone she looked over to Cookie. "Cookie." Was her one-word greeting given with only a slight nod of recognition.

"Hello, Maria, you believe this son of yours? In the hospital, again!"

Another female voice cracked through the now busying conversation.

"Oh God! Are you okay? You were all over the news this morning!" It was Molly, she quickly squeezed her way past the other women to Tommy's bedside, leaving a tired looking Jack Norris standing in the doorway. "Can I—can I, is it okay?" Molly began asking, but before there was an answer, she bent over the bed and embraced and kissed Tommy passionately and several times, as Tommy just lay in bed, somewhat dumbfounded at just how busy his room had gotten in the last three minutes.

"Thank God you're safe, oh my God, thank God you're safe," Molly continued, truly shaken at the sight of Tommy in his bed, her hand gently placed on the left side of his face she looked deeply into his eyes as she repeated herself, "Thank God, thank God you're safe."

Cookie looked at the scene between Molly and Tommy, with a scowl on her face, wondering who this twenty something beauty was that was gushing all over her ex-husband. "She's a child" she said softly and with a hint of jealousy, but just loud enough for Caitlin, and Maria to hear. Maria smiling while giving Cookie the side eye, happy at the way this was playing out.

"I'm fine, Molly, actually feeling pretty good," Tommy replied, slightly taken aback by this onslaught of attention, "Molly, this is my mother, Maria, her sister, my aunt Sophie. My, my ex-wife, Cookie, my daughter, Caitlin, my Partner Doreen, and my boss, Kevin. Everybody, this is Molly."

A group reply, "Hi, hello, Molly" followed.

"And that handsome, and silent man, in the doorway there is Jack."

Then another group "Hi. Hello, Jack."

Just as Jack reciprocated with a "Hello everyone," he was gently pushed to the side as little Roya entered the room. She wore a grave and nervous look on her face and was much more subdued than the rest of the ladies who had just entered the room.

"Oh, man." She said lowly, but not so low not to be heard, she slowly made her way over to Tommy's bedside and leaned in and hugged him. She didn't kiss him as the others did, and there was no passion, as there was with Cookie and Molly, but she hung on tighter, longer, and harder than anyone else in the room. As she straightened herself up, she lowly said, "I'm sorry." As she wiped a tear from her cheek with her wrist.

Tommy reached up with his right hand and placed it on her cheek, "It's okay, I'm fine, I'm gonna be just fine, and it comes with the territory, kid."

For a moment a silence hung over the room. There was something odd about this interaction, something personal that everyone else picked up on, but no one had a clue what it could be.

Tommy then spoke up and broke that silence.

"For those of you who don't know her already, this is Roya--Roya, you of course know my mother, this is her sister, my aunt Sophie, this is my partner Doreen, my boss Kevin … You remember Cookie and Caitlin of course, and this is Molly and Jack, who you may know from Bailey's Corner?"

Again, there was a slight moment of odd silence. Then Cookie, who had a strange look on her face after what had just transpired between Molly and Tommy and what followed between Roya and Tommy, immediately stepped forward and embraced Roya,

"Of course, Roya, my God, it's been so long, look at how beautiful you've become." Caitlin followed her mother and gave Roya a huge hug,

"Oh my God, Roya!"

As the pleasantries began to go back and forth, Caitlin's boyfriend, Nick, appeared in the doorway, somewhat befuddled by the large crowd, and the volume the room had reached, not to mention the uniformed police officer guarding the door, which he did not expect to see. Nick just stood silently.

"And everyone this is Nick, my Caitlin's boyfriend."

Another collective "Hi, hello, Nick" came from the now nine people who were standing around Tommy's bed.

As the ladies all began to speak at one another in unison, they were interrupted by Detective Schaffer, and two other detectives, entering the now crowded room.

"Hello, excuse me, may we have a moment with Detective Keane, please just a moment, official police business." Schaffer spoke loudly, trying to be heard above all the voices swirling around the room.

Slightly startled, everyone, but Lieutenant Bricks and Doreen, exited the room and made their way to the floors visitor's lounge.

Detective Schaffer closed the door, "Okay, so we just got word from the 109 Squad in Queens. They located two young, Chinese, gang members dead, dumped in a dumpster outside of a housing project there – both had the same headless dragon tattoo on their chest that our other guy had, both were shot several times in the head and face with .9mm rounds – one had two .38 special nyclad rounds in him, one in his shoulder and one in his hip."

Li Jun

"Looks like the Purple Dragons wanted to clean up after themselves just after failing to take you out, Tom." Lieutenant Bricks said flatly.

"Yes, sir, that's exactly what it looks like, Lieutenant," Schaffer replied, "They also recovered the Honda nearby. From what I understand, there are some detectives, and FBI, making their way up here to interview you themselves. Detective Keane – Lieutenant, I may have to get ahold of you to cross a couple of t's or dot an i, or two, but as far as I'm concerned, this is a closed case with the White Plains Police Department. We wish you nothing but the best and a speedy recovery, Detective Keane."

"Thanks, Schaffer, I appreciate it." Tommy replied.

"Yes, Detective, thank you. If ever we can do anything for you, please let me know." Lieutenant Bricks added.

Over the next few hours, the above-mentioned people, came and went, along with nurses and doctors coming in to monitor Tommy and check his vitals from time to time.

Slowly, one by one, everyone said their goodbye's. Lieutenant Bricks and Doreen, drove Maria, Sophia, and Roya, back to the city in their squad car. As the afternoon turned to evening, Tommy was again alone in his room.

He didn't realize it at the time, but the show of support given to him by his family, and friends, had, at least for the moment, alleviated that feeling of loneliness that had hit him the weeks before, and he was feeling quite happy.

It was passed visiting hours when he heard a woman's voice speaking to the uniformed officer stationed at Tommy's door, it was Lisa Yan.

"Hey, Tommy, how you feeling? I'm sorry it took me so long to make it up here, but it was a busy, busy day," she paused, then wiped a tear from her eye, "Oh my God, look at you, I am so sorry, I didn't see any of this coming, oh Tommy... "

"Shhh, Lisa, I'm fine, I'm fine. This is part of what we do, I'm here, right? So that makes today a good day."

The two of them talked about the case for a bit, then Lisa said goodbye and left, and Tommy fell into a deep sleep.

Sometime after midnight, the elevator door opened and a man in an old, tired and stained trench coat stepped out and slowly made his way towards Tommy's room, he paused and noticed the young, uniformed police officer leaning on the counter of the nurse's station, making conversation with one of the duty nurses.

The man walked up and into Tommy's room without notice from the police officer or the nurse he was chatting up.

It was Mark Stein. Stein was unable to make it up earlier than he had because of work and prior commitments, he stood silently over Tommy for a few minutes as he slept, he placed his hand on Tommy's forearm, gently, so not to wake him.

"Zei gezunt, my friend." Said Mark, in a hushed whisper, then turned and walked out of Tommy's room and back to the elevator, never being detected by the police officer or the nurse, who were still deep in conversation.

Li Jun

Chapter Twenty-Three

Tommy was released from the hospital two days later and placed on sick leave for the next four weeks. During this time, Lisa had continued tying up loose ends with a few more arrests, and with more planned as the mountain of information that had been forwarded to her was deciphered.

The messages Roya was receiving dwindled to nothing shortly after Lisa had made her big sweep and most of the Purple Dragons were picked up.

Min had been moved to a new hotel and was under the watch of detectives assigned to the District Attorney's office.

The other members of B Squad continued to catch cases as usual only slightly more as they were temporarily short one detective.

Two days after leaving the hospital Tommy made his way down to the City Morgue. He was able to meet with Medical Examiner Smyth and find out the details on Li Jun's remains. He had called around, and found a burial plot in Putnam County, and he had decided that he would do whatever he had to do to take possession of Li's body and give her a dignified burial. The thought of her being placed in a numbered wooden box, and stacked in a mass grave in potter's field out on Hart Island was something he simply couldn't stand the thought of.

He made the arrangements over the following week, and with his own money, purchased the plot, a casket, and a small headstone which he had written, "Here lies Li Jun, May She Rest in Peace."

He never mentioned this to anyone in the police department, or to his family. He made the decision and arrangements on his own, and the only two people to ever see this grave were he and Min, who he drove up to the cemetery several weeks after Li had been buried.

Epilogue

Mama and Peter Woo did indeed escape capture. They had first made it to Toronto, as was assumed, then they flew to Taiwan under false names with new passports. To this day, they still operate as human traffickers and drug smugglers. Although they are less respected, and their operations are less profitable than they once were, their income is believed to be in the millions annually.

Detective Lisa Yan went on to arrest dozens of other Purple Dragons, as well as members of other gangs, due to the information she had received and translated off those mysterious flash drives that had shown up again and again at her office. Her related investigations solved thirteen open murder cases and shut down one of the largest sex trafficking rings in the Northeast. Eighteen months after the start of operation Dragon Killer, due to its overwhelming success, Lisa was promoted to Detective Second grade. Detective Yan is still in the NYPD and still assigned to the Asian Gang Unit.

Marty Chu was subsequently charged in eight murder cases, along with a slew of drug, weapons, and extortion charges. He eventually turned State's evidence and testified against the Woos, who were tried in absentia. He received a reduced sentence of eighteen years, which he is currently serving in the Clinton Correctional Facility, in Dannemora, New York.

Li Jun

Tony Chu was charged in six murders, as well as for numerous lesser crimes. He too turned State's evidence against the Woos for a lighter sentence and is also serving eighteen years. He is currently serving time in Downstate Correctional Facility, in Fishkill, New York.

Teddy Lo, was charged with over one hundred felony counts, involving the promotion of prostitution and assault. Teddy was implicated in two homicides, for which he was never formally charged, he is currently serving twelve years in Downstate Correctional Facility.

Min, gave testimony in both City and Federal court, against the Woos, the Chu's, and Teddy Lo, as well as numerous other gang members. She was relocated to a suburb outside of a small city in Florida, where she eventually married a man thirty years her senior, her husband treats her well, and she now lives a stable and comfortable life.

Noel Fitsimmons, gave testimony against Mama Woo, as to the murder of Li Jun, he continues to work with his father at the D&B liquor store on 2nd Avenue.

Detective Lisa Yan's investigation uncovered many improprieties and violations that bordered criminality regarding the career of FBI agent Michelle Kai. Agent Kai however was never arrested for any criminal activity, nor was she fired. She was, however, removed from her post in New York, demoted, and transferred to a field office in Kansas City, where she still works to this day.

Congressman Ethan Swalstein was surrounded by scandal after his involvement with the Woos was brought to light by Gil Nunez, and the national press got ahold of it. He did run for reelection, however, bowed out when it became painfully obvious, he would not be able to win his primary election due to the fallout of his story. Ethan Swalstein now works as a real estate lawyer on Long Island.

All of this, however, remains in the future. Currently, we all await Detective Tommy Keane to wake to the same routine and see what new case will come his way when he returns to the 2-1.

Author's Note

Human trafficking, and sex slavery are a major problem worldwide. It is estimated that more than 30,000 children die annually in sex trafficking around the world, and as many as 300,000 underage girls, are sold for sex in America alone, every year.

As of the writing of this book, the US Department of State, ranks China as a tier three country. Meaning it does not meet the minimum standards for the elimination of trafficking and is not making significant efforts to do so.

Tier three is the lowest, and the worst, rating of the three tiers used to describe the efforts put forth by a nation to curb the trafficking of human beings.

The Drug Enforcement Agency (DEA) assesses China as the primary country of origin for illicit fentanyl and fentanyl-related substances trafficked into the United States. They also find Chinese drug gangs 'primary partner's' in the smuggling trade, with the Mexican cartels, who smuggle every sort of narcotic imaginable across the southern border into the US annually grossing over sixty-four billion dollars a year.

It is also believed that seventy percent of human trafficking victims, regardless of country of origin, enter the United States via its southern border with Mexico, fifty percent of those individuals being minors.

Read on for a sneak peek at the next book in the Tommy Keane series:

Sol Abromowitz

The three detectives arrive on scene: the south side of East 66th Street about twenty feet west of York Avenue. Patrol had already taped off the corner with police tape and they are met by Sergeant Diaz, as they approach.

"Detective Keane, good to see you back pal, how you feelin'?"

"Feelin' good, Sarge, how you been?"

"Been good, been real good. Just found out we're having another kid, and I couldn't be happier." He grinned.

"Really? Good for you man."

"This one yours, Keane?"

"No sir, my good friend here, Clay, will be taking this one." Tommy nodded toward the man standing next to him.

Sergeant Diaz stuck his hand out and nodded his head, "Detective."

"How you doin', Sergeant Diaz? Clay, Clay Johnson." As the two men shook hands.

"Good to meet you, Clay – and how are you, Doreen?" Sergeant Diaz asked, turning himself to the side to get a look at Doreen around Clay's broad frame.

"Doing good, Sarge, better than that poor fella on the sidewalk over there, that's for sure."

"What do we know so far?" Clay asked.

"Elderly male, Jewish, looks and sounds like he took a couple whacks with some sort of blunt weapon. We have two witnesses for you, I'm happy to say, both have the same description, but are real weak on any details. They both say it just happened too fast."

"How you know he's Jewish?" Clay asked.

"He's wearing a yarmulke, so I took a guess… come take a look."

The three detectives slipped under the police tape and stood around the body. Each took a moment and stared at the victim, a tall, white haired, older gentleman, in a black nylon overcoat, and a dark navy suit. A navy yarmulke was pinned atop his head with hairpins. A broken pair of horned rimmed glasses still on his face and his brown eyes open behind them. Two gashes were on his forehead, and neither appeared to be caused by his fall to the sidewalk.

"You bag the hands?" Clay asked.

"Yep." Sergeant Diaz answered.

"Thanks."

Clay and Tommy both donned some latex gloves and began a search of the body, Clay immediately reached into the dead gentleman's rear pocket and retrieved his wallet.

"Solomon Abramowitz looks like he's... 79 years old, lives a couple of blocks over on 64th Street."

Tommy pulled a small bundle of bills from Mr. Abramowitz's front right pants pocket, "$56 Dollars."

Tommy ran his hand around the back of the victim's head and found another gash, raising his bloody hand to show Clay and Doreen.

"Whatever he was hit with opened up the back of his head pretty good, too."

Then the three of them paused for a moment, and again all stared down at Mr. Abramowitz, then all simultaneously at the surroundings.

"Doesn't look like a robbery, what you guys think?"

"Maybe a robbery gone wrong?" Doreen answered.

Li Jun

About the Authors

Travis Myers and Natasha Myers Marsiguerra are a brother and sister team who both grew up in New York City.

Travis is a retired New York City Police Detective, and Natasha works for the IBEW (International Brotherhood of Electrical Workers) Local 234 in California.

Together they form a perfect team in that Travis, who has more stories to tell than a pub full of Irishmen, suffers from dyslexia and abhors anything to do with reading or writing. Natasha, his beloved little sister, is an avid reader of absolutely anything that is put in front of her and has been blessed with the gift of gab. She can out-story just about anyone, in any room, at any given time, and she can also type 60 words per minute. More importantly, Natasha is able to understand where her older brother is coming from, and craft his stories into a readable format.

Together, they weave the Tommy Keane Detective series into well-braided fictional tales that are nearly all based in actual events that they, and their friends and relatives, have lived. Travis and Natasha deliver on their promise to tell gritty, honest stories that are rooted in the everyday lives of everyday people.

Printed in the USA
CPSIA information can be obtained
at www.ICGtesting.com
JSHW022226060923
47952JS00007B/24